PRAISE FOR SHADOW OF THE CITY

"A police procedural set in one of the snazziest fantasy settings ever."

— Rachel Neumeier, author of *The Floating Islands*

"A fun fantasy mystery featuring a vibrant, inclusive world and a deep friendship between the protagonist and her partner sleuth. If you'd like a diverting escape to lift your spirits, Rocío and Hala have just the adventure for you."

— Courtney Schafer, author of the Shattered Sigil trilogy

"A fun, sometimes serious novel that blends humor, mystery and magic beautifully."

— A. T. Greenblatt, Nebula Award-winning author of "Give The Family My Love"

RIVER OF LIES

R. MORGAN

Cover design by

Version 1

The Fourth Gorgon press

New York, NY

CHAPTER 1

Rocío FOLDED her arms and surveyed the Plaza de la ciudad, or at least what she could see of it. The week-long midsummer market currently blanketed the enormous acreage of the plaza, and they stood three stalls deep into the housewares section. "I need to get a present for my parents' contract renewal party," she told Hala, her friend, fellow detective at the Miraflores Community Justice Center and her partner. As they had off this Saturday at the end of January, only the first label was important today.

"Here?" Hala asked, raising an eyebrow at their surroundings. An ice cream slick, three wailing children and two overwhelmed parents had diverted them from the more direct route to the magic exhibit and the tacata contest. On their left, stacks of metal colanders, serving bowls and salt shakers winked in the sun, while a musta-chioed man on the right shook out cotton hand towels printed with bright yellow flowers for a prospective customer. The air smelled of popcorn, barbecuing meat and the dusky-sharp scent of roasting poblanos.

Hala touched one careful finger to a metal nutmeg grinder stamped with flowers. "While you could easily find something for my parents here, your mother would kill you if you bought her anything so plebeian and then I'd have to resign so I didn't have to arrest her."

Rocío was briefly distracted by wondering if Hala would resign if she faced that moral dilemma. She didn't think so. It was more likely that Hala would happily arrest Rocío's mother, not just for that hypothetical filicide but for a litany of very real offenses against Rocío over the years. "I was thinking about a comal." She pointed with her elbow at a very nice display of griddles, cooking pans and pots.

"Do they even know what a comal is for? Surely the cook makes the tortillas, not your parents. Have they ever even been in their kitchen?" Hala patted sweat from her forehead with a folded handkerchief and pushed her fingers through her short dark hair, making it stand up even more. The press of bodies made the hot day even hotter. She edged between two women with bulging red and white canvas bags. Against Hala's forest green vest and unbleached linen shorts, the bags made a very festive picture.

Rocío stubbornly refused to follow and stepped closer to the comal. The vendor advanced on her.

"They've renewed their marriage contract almost every five years for decades. I've run out of gift ideas. I'm getting desperate."

"Remind me if I'm wrong—"

Rocío rolled her eyes. Hala was never wrong when she admitted she might be.

"—but isn't this a special renewal year?"

"Fifty years, if you don't count those five years when my mother married that politician and failed to produce any offspring. Or thirty-eight if you only count the years without simultaneous marriage contracts to anyone else. And twenty if you count the contracts that stipulated monogamy. Imagine, twenty years of monogamy." Rocío frowned at a salt and pepper shaker set in the shape of two round bodies hugging each other.

"Señorx, let me—" the vendor began persuasively.

"Not that. She's not buying." Hala hooked her arm through Rocío's and steered her through a gap in the crowd. "At least look in the textiles section. I heard they have some cross-woven Jeen silk."

Rocío left the housewares without any regret. She had been kidding. Mostly. Her exasperation with her parents was all too real, however. "Is that what you're getting your parents?"

Both their parents had married on 12 February, though Hala's parents in 399 after the founding of the city of La Beneficia de nuestros vecinos y los seres celestiales (La Bene for short) and Rocío's in 444 and 439 and a few other years as each short-term marriage contract came up for renewal. Rocío had lost track on purpose, one of her small acts of defiance that made her feel like she was maintaining some distance from her parents. The marriage anniversary was one of those coincidences that had helped both Rocío and Hala reach out in friendship when they were first partnered together at the CJC seven years ago.

Hala stopped short. Rocío followed her line of sight to a short frazzled woman in front of a chemist's stall. She wore the loose bronze sarong secured with a sash through the legs and thick gold earrings of the river folk. Her mousy brown hair was braided close to her scalp. All of that made her stand out.

The chemist leaned across the counter and stabbed an aggressive finger at the woman and then at the medicines displayed in glass bottles and little cardboard boxes. The river woman lifted pleading hands. The chemist, a typical Benerex woman with dark brown eyes and dark hair looped up and secured with twinkling metal pins, shook her head and pinned something in place on the counter with her hand.

The river woman backed up. Her hand flashed out, snagging something else. She spun on her heel and dashed away.

The chemist, outraged, shouted, "Thief!"

Rocío didn't need Hala's logic skills to see where the thief would have to run; her own spatial skills were pretty good after seven years on the stage and another seven in the CJC. There was a gap where a vendor had failed to show up, and beyond that there was only one more ring of stalls and then the comparatively empty plaza itself, where the thief could lose herself among people enjoying the day and not be hemmed in by stalls.

Rocío surged forward, blocking the gap just as the thief careened into it. She bounced off Rocío. Hala boxed in the thief from behind.

The young woman glared at Rocío and put her hands on her hips. Weird behavior for a thief. She was shaking though.

"You have no right," the woman said, her voice throttled with anger and a slight accent. "Get out of my way."

"You've been accused of theft," Rocío said, recovering from this unexpected opening sally. "We're detectives from the Miraflores CJC, so we do have the right."

"Yeah? Go ahead, ask what I've stolen."

A crowd had gathered around them and now they murmured with a nasty undercurrent. Just a few months ago, a foreigner had used imported magic to infect people in the city with malaria, and since then foreigners had been the target of a few assaults. The malarial mosquito fairies had scarred the psyche of the city, and that didn't just go away. This could turn ugly quickly.

Rocío looked past Hala, expecting to see the chemist hovering nearby to demand the return of her property, but she was still behind her counter, half turned away with her arms folded, and not looking in their direction. Weird behavior for a business owner. The weirdnesses were just piling up. Rocío lifted her chin in a signal to Hala, who considered the shaking woman and then turned to the chemist.

"I'm not leaving my stall! What if there are others like her, just waiting to steal more?"

"She has a point—"

"Of course she does, she's Benerex like you," the river woman broke in hotly.

"—about her wares," Rocío finished calmly, not matching the rising emotions. "Will you come back so we can get to the bottom of this?"

The river woman raked the crowd with a scathing glance. "Do I have a choice?" She stalked stiffly back to the stall. The crowd barely let her through.

"Come on," Rocío said, "give us some room."

A few people stepped back, pressing into the bystanders behind them. Rocío could tell they weren't going to leave, so she didn't undermine her perceived authority by trying to make them, but she began to worry about riots and mayhem and melees. It had been almost three weeks since the last riot and the city was finally calming down. Before that, periodic waves of hysteria had swept the city, fed by the less reputable newspapers and people's reasonable fears. And also a few times when someone spooked because a pigeon that looked like a MMF flew by.

"What are you accusing this woman of stealing?" Rocío asked the chemist.

"Why, that quinine she has in her hand! Enough malaria medication to dose a school." The chemist jutted her head forward belligerently.

It had to be quinine.

Another ugly grumble rippled through the crowd. Rocío put her hand up, gesturing for quiet. "It is still malaria season."

"It's a lie! I didn't steal it." The river woman's voice shook with tension, her back stiff with outrage and fear. "It's enough for one person. And I paid for it, a whole Ka sol, because she wouldn't tell me the price, wouldn't sell it to me even though I could see it sitting right there and my family needs it. A Ka sol should buy enough quinine to dose a school." She took a deep breath and spoke more calmly. "She can't have too many coins from the Ka Empire."

"And that's probably fake! You know what these boat traders are! She's hoarding or means to murder us all in our sleep."

Unfortunately, Rocío could follow this brand of illogical logic. People *had* hoarded malaria medication and chemists *had* raised their prices sky high until the governor intervened.

"On the contrary, Señorx," Hala said, "Hoarding has not been a problem for almost two months. There is enough malaria medication for everyone, especially as the normal malaria season is half over. You do remember that it's a crime to deny anyone lifesaving medicines, don't you? And that you could lose your license?"

"She's not people!"

The river woman fell back a step, her face going as grey as her vest. Rocío scanned the crowd, looking for fellow advocates, trustworthy familiar faces or anyone who could help if the worst happened. A man in a Ya loincloth and cape wisely disappeared down one of the aisles. The majority of people stayed, looking angry, though a few seemed merely curious.

"That's enough," Hala said sharply.

5

"You can't expect me to—" the chemist appealed to the crowd.

In a quieter voice, Hala said, "If you incite a riot, I won't have to arrest you because we'll all be dead."

The chemist looked around uncertainly.

One man muttered, "I'm not dying on her word," and elbowed his way out of the crowd. A few more people left. Too many stayed.

A man who had been buying a tincture from the chemist put down the glass vial with a click and stepped away. "It's true, the woman did try to pay, but she," he pointed at the chemist, "wouldn't take her money." A few more people, maybe the speaker's friends or family, shifted away from the chemist, physical distancing reflecting their emotional distancing.

The river woman's expression seemed to struggle with itself: incredulity that anyone was standing up for her, resentment that they had to, and relief.

An anonymous voice shouted agreement. Rocío sighed to herself at this evidence of human nature. So it was okay to act like someone wasn't a person, but it wasn't okay to say so out loud. *I guess it's progress, when people internalize that as unacceptable behavior. I'll take it.* She could feel the mood of the crowd turning and her pulse slowed. They were less likely to riot now.

"Señorx," Hala said to the chemist, "I was going to give the two of you a summons to the adjudicator to rule on the accusation of theft, but now—"

"A summons?" the chemist cried wrathfully. "She won't be here. She's a vagrant, they're all vagrants."

This time no one called out in support. A few more people left, looking shamefaced.

"But now I'm going to fine you for disturbing the peace," Hala finished. She raised her voice and addressed the spectators. "Who will do their civic duty and appear as witnesses? More, who will uphold La Bene's reputation? I can't catch you all before you disappear into the market, but do we want our city to be known as inhospitable and prejudiced?" Hala could do a bit of acting of her own when she wanted to.

Several people stepped forward. Hala took a summons pad out of one of her many pockets and started writing. Of course she had a summons pad on her day off. The chemist tried to retreat behind her counter and Hala blocked her. "I will look for the Ka Sol first."

The thin paper of a summons crackled as Hala passed it to Rocío, who passed it to the river woman. "This is for tomorrow. When you go to that address, they'll tell you what day to return for the adjudication. Will you be in La Bene long enough to testify? It would help. You might get your money back."

The woman clutched the medicine to her chest. "How long?"

"A few days at least."

The woman's gaze flickered nervously between Rocío and the people around them. "Probably. I, uh, I have to go."

"How do we get in contact with you?"

"I'm Pilar of *The Resolute*. That's my boat. We're docked at the upriver piers."

"Rocío," Hala called. She held up a gold coin. "She had only one."

The chemist glared, the muscles in her forearms twitching as she repeatedly clenched her hands.

"That's in your favor," Rocío told Pilar. "If you need anything, I'm Detective Díaz and that's Detective Haddad. We're in the Miraflores Community Justice Center on the Plaza de los mártires. It's all on the summons."

Pilar looked like she was going to say something but the chemist started arguing with Hala. Pilar flinched back and scuttled away.

"I'll protest to the adjudicator," the chemist said. "I know my rights."

"You do that," Hala said placidly. "You're still getting a summons." She ripped off the summons and, when the chemist didn't accept it, placed it on the counter and weighted it down with the discarded glass vial. As soon as Hala's back was turned the chemist made an obscene gesture.

"She had the coin in her pocket." Hala said as she joined Rocío. She wiped her hands on her shorts. "Three more people came forward as witnesses."

"Good old appearances," Rocío said. "They'll testify at the hearing to show each other they're not like that, it's just other people who are ignorant and prejudiced."

"If it works in our favor, I won't protest too much. Did you get her name?"

"And her boat's name, which is as good as a surname, just before she disappeared. I told her she'd probably get her money back."

"We might see her again on that account."

They stopped at a water station for Hala to wash her hands. Though she never actually complained about putting her hands in other people's pockets, Rocío knew Hala didn't like doing body searches. Rocío checked her pocket watch. The metal chain and the watch case were warm, indistinguishable from the heat of the day or her own body heat. "We still have time before the tacata competition."

"Good." Hala shook water from her hands, ignoring the limp towel provided for that purpose. She led them purposefully, though they still stopped to look at a cascade purple orchids, dark red cosmos and cheery yellow poppies, all so cleverly done in paper that from a distance they looked real and for Rocío to quiz a bookseller about whether he had the scripts for the biggest performances of the upcoming theater season and when he would get them. But they reached the exposition section for magic machines with plenty of time.

A few years ago an automobile had been the talk of the market and soon after the CJC had somehow acquired one. It was hard to drive and had a tendency to explode (so far no one had been hurt) but was useful on occasion when horses, bicycles or carriages weren't fast enough and need outweighed caution. As a result, Rocío and Hala liked to keep an eye on the more extravagant inventions. Which wasn't to say they were all bad; electric lights powered by the magic of La Bene had first been shown at the summer market when Rocío was about eighteen, and now they were a reliable and ubiquitous feature of life. More recently someone had invented a recorder small enough to be useful for advocates and they were still stumbling through the implications for their work.

Rocío was an indifferent magic user; Hala was better, but the CJC had professional magickers who had gone to University for forensics and other practical things. In La Bene magic manifested as electrical energy, an extension of the body's electric field beyond its bounds and under conscious control. In school, everyone learned to warm their tea and to not accidentally give others electrical shocks.

A trolley that didn't look that different from those already in use in La Bene had pride of space on the very edge of the market, possibly because it was the biggest contraption in sight. It didn't have the usual hookups for horses so probably it had an internal engine like the automobile. Rocío shuddered. That was a tragedy waiting to happen if it worked as well as the auto.

In front of one of the other exhibits, a bunch of people with sashes over their wrap dresses were shaking aprons and chanting. One of the men stepped to the side, giving Rocío a clear view of the signs planted in front of them.

"Launderers demand official employment re-education" and "We remember the lightkeepers." A quarter of a century ago, lightkeepers were employed to light the oil street lamps of the city and deliver wood, coal and oil for home use. Then lights powered by magic were invented and the vast majority of lightkeepers were very quickly unemployed. A few had the magic skills to transition into the new job and taught others, but without the University certificate for their magic level it was hard for them to compete with the wave of new, younger workers, who had gone to University.

"Do you see any advocates?" Rocío asked, still thinking about mobs and riots.

"No."

They lingered on the edges, assessing the mood of the crowd. Just as Rocío concluded her initial worry was lingering adrenaline, Hala said, "Not every crowd becomes a mob."

"They seem more business-like than anything," Rocío said.

The group shifted again like a school of fish, and Rocío saw the object of their protest. As was the current fashion, the metal machine resembled an animal, in this case a sheep with a barrel for a body and a suggestion of a face in the mechanism on one end, and a lever on the other for a tail. The sign said "Automatic clothes washer."

Another group with their aprons still on huddled around a man and a woman with exhibitor tags. They had the air of conducting intense negotiations.

"If we go into partnership," one of the launderers was saying, "you can install your machines in the laundries we already own and our customers will become your customers. You will have an assured demand." She gestured at herself and the other launderers. "Between us we have decades of experience."

"Centuries."

"But—" the female exhibitor protested, possibly with air castle images of her future status as a wealthy monopolist disappearing before her eyes.

The eloquent launderer scratched his chin. "Have you considered the different water temperatures and rotation speeds needed to wash different fabrics? We can help you with research and development. After all, we are the experts."

"That is a design challenge we haven't been able to solve," the male exhibitor said to his colleague.

"I want a closer look," Hala said, stepping closer.

Rocío usually wasn't as intrigued by machines as Hala, but she could see the potential of an appliance that could do laundry. Hala probably appreciated it even more as her large family generated mountains of dirty clothes every week. Rocío hung back, staying clear of the crowd. The adrenaline still pumping through her veins made her twitchy.

Hala, the exhibitor and the launderers talked animatedly for a few minutes. Grinning, Hala returned. "Intriguing! I got his card. This is finally starting to feel like a day off."

Rocío grinned back at her. "You've had your turn. Now it's mine." She took Hala's arm and pointed them west. "It's time to dance."

CHAPTER 2

A FEW DAYS LATER, Rocío's so-called friends were ganging up on her.

In the late afternoon, the big open room of the Community Justice Center was remarkably quiet, with the exception of Isis's diatribe. Isis Soler Ibáñez was statuesque and taller than the average Benerex, with dark hair with one lock of gray on her right temple, and magnetic, whether she was giving a speech in the House of Refugees to the government of La Bene or trying to convince Rocío her view of her parents was distorted. Next to her, Hala's quiet reserve and slightly sharp, darker face seemed more pronounced.

Isis sat on Rocío's desk, the pens, folders and photograph of Rocío's nonna pushed to one side, and one sandaled foot on the seat of Rocío's chair, holding her in place. As the chair was already pushed back as far as it would go against the next desk, Rocío thought it an admirable psychological tactic, though she wished it weren't being used against her. Hala tapped a pen against the one folder centered on her desk, her eyebrows scrunched down over her thoughtful dark eyes, her silence tacit agreement.

"You don't have to go," Isis said in her most persuasive voice, the one she used on politicians in the opposition party and her children when she needed them to do something they didn't want to do. "You've gone to every one of their contract signing parties. They've been renewing their marriage for fifty years, surely you deserve a break."

Rocío wanted to put her hands over her ears, and she would have if she were home—she would have left if she were home, but that was the whole point of them confronting her here. It was harder to escape and her evasion tactics were limited by the need to maintain professionalism in the workplace. Besides, even if she covered her ears, she'd hear all the adjectives Isis wasn't saying this time: *ridiculous* parties, *perdido* marriage. *Evil* parents. Isis had never hidden her opinion of Rocío's parents, and Rocío knew very well that one of Isis's many attractions was that she said things Rocío would never allow herself to think, much less say.

It was easy for Isis and Hala to abide by cultural norms of family responsibility, duty and cohesion because their families were mostly pleasant, and easy for them to think Rocío could defy more of those norms because she had already defied so many of them. Rocío had found the opposite to be true.

"Surely that's an argument for why I should go," Rocío said as reasonably as she could manage. She recharged Hala's fan with a little spark of her magic so it wouldn't run down and nudged it so it blew the hot office air more directly at her and a little less at Isis. "It will cause an argument if I don't go." She thought about caressing Isis's ankle to distract her and discarded the idea. It was cheap, and she didn't like to bring sex into the workplace. It wouldn't distract Hala anyway.

"That's both circular logic and a sunk costs fallacy," Hala said.

"It will cause an argument if you do go," Isis said. "You know it's true, they always pick a fight with you." She held up a hand. "I know what you're going to say. Maybe they can't help it, but you can certainly change what you do." Her even tones slipped and she looked to Hala for help, even nudging Rocío's chair in that direction.

"Isis is right. You know what will happen. They'll summon you, demanding your assistance and then not let you do anything. They'll criticize what you wear. They'll insult your job and life choices and introduce you to people who would love to do your parents the favor of giving you a job. And then one of them will start a fight with you and blame you for it."

"It's her father's turn," Isis offered.

"And then you'll be upset and depressed for days and you'll spend all your spare time swimming and your friends will worry that you'll drown from exhaustion."

Isis nodded. "It's true." She spun Rocío's chair back to face her. "My dear friend, why don't you come have dinner with me and my spouses? Tano and Jacinta would love to see you and so would the children. You could stay the night in the peace and quiet of the country-side. You like to read the children stories. We could even perform one of he plays we were in together, so long ago." Isis's voice gained real enthusiasm, and that was harder to resist than the badgering. Isis had been a constant in Rocío's life since her theater days, even as their relationship changed to accommodate spouses and other lovers and children and changed again. Rocío was one of the reasons Isis's marriage contracts never included monogamy clauses, though not the only one.

Hala was watching Rocío like a hawk for any sign of weakening. She wasn't going to get it. Rocío knew what her duty to her family was, and she'd been doing it for forty-three years. She had defied them in the one way that mattered, by becoming a performer and then a detective, and so was dutiful in every other way to make it up to them and uphold her responsibilities. In any case, they were her family and one did not abandon one's family. That way lay social dissolution and chaos.

She was aware that her thoughts were getting rather overwrought and that she wasn't going to be able to answer Isis in any convincing way.

The heavy scent of roses in full bloom drifted through the open doors onto the interior courtyard. In the silence the buzz of bees and the whir of fans was suddenly loud.

She was saved by her favorite chaski, Paco. They weren't supposed to have favorites among the teenaged message runners serving voca-tional apprenticeships in the hopes of being officially hired when they were old enough, but everyone did. Paco's determination to escape the place allowed to him by birth and luck reminded her of herself. He still wasn't running, though this time it wasn't entirely the brace on his broken leg that slowed him down. He also had a pitcher of tea in one hand, a small metal bucket of ice in the other, and a clipboard tucked under his elbow.

"I brought tea," he said loudly, interrupting. "With ice." He didn't quite dare try to displace Isis from Rocío's desk, so he put everything on Hala's and brandished the clipboard at her with a censuring frown. "You have to sign."

They were lucky to have ice, a luxury imported from the western mountains, packed in sawdust, transported across the vast plains by wagon and boat, and stored in the coolest and deepest room at the CJC. It was maybe the one good contribution of their chief, a political appointee with family connections and little concern for actually doing his job. Apparently he couldn't live without cool beverages in the summer heat. The clipboard system was this year's effort to cut down accusations of unfair use, ice peculation and hoarding. The attempts at hoarding would have been amusing if it hadn't wasted so much ice and soured the chief's disposition.

Hala frowned back at Paco in a measuring way. He held his ground and stared back. Isis laughed, the sound full and amused. She finally dropped her foot from Rocío's chair and poured the tea into glasses she pulled out of Rocío's desk. She handed one to Paco and clinked her glass against his. This time he blushed so hard it was visible on his dark skin. He gulped down tea and choked.

Rocío thumped his back and whispered thanks. "Hala, we should go talk to Señorx Phrompan. He's pretty sure it was Señorx Iversen who killed his rooster." To Isis, she said, "When it's not riots, it's been the summer of livestock complaints. Goats in gardens, pigs loose in the streets, roosters that crow all night."

"The pig incident made it all the way to the House of Refuges. We spent an entire session debating livestock control in the city," Isis said affably enough, but with a glint in her eye that said she wasn't giving up on the topic of Rocío's parents. Not that Rocío thought she would, but any reprieve was a good reprieve.

"Ministrx Soler is sitting on my report." Hala tugged the folder out from under Isis's butt, making Rocío snort at Hala's trademark combination of formality and informality with Isis.

An unknown chaski skidded to a stop just inside the entrance to the room and then advanced on them. She had wispy light-brown hair and plump cheeks like a baby's, and Rocío couldn't read her badge from this distance. Rocío wondered idly where the advocate on desk duty had gone. Even chaskis weren't supposed to wander that freely into the back part of the CJC.

"Sanblas CJC," Paco whispered to Rocío. The Sanblas district ran along the eastern bank of Río ja' mayu, the river that cut through La Bene generally northwest to southeast. The district included everything from the docks, to the warehouses, to permanent businesses and itinerant vendors that supported the riverine and maritime trade.

"Thanks."

"Detective Díaz?" The chaski's eyes moved uncertainly between Rocío and Hala. Rocío noted with amusement that she didn't even consider Isis as a possible officer of the law. Of course Isis *was* a ministrx, one of those august people who created the law and passed on instructions on how to enforce it to people like Rocío.

"That's me," Rocío said, half waving. "What's up?"

The girl glanced longingly at the fan. Sweat glistened on her face and neck. "Message from Advocate Silvia Dante Ruíz."

Rocío pointed the fan towards the chaski, who sighed with pleasure and moved directly into the cooler air, even more of her wispy hair escaping its pins. "I don't recognize the name." Rocío put out her hand for the expected slip of paper.

"It's a verbal message," the chaski said apologetically. "Advocate Silvia's out at the docks now—it's urgent. She says she needs your expertise. She was just promoted from chaski." Pride mixed with hope for her own future mixed in her voice.

Rocío covered her surprise with a sip of tea. Hala rubbed her nose. At Miraflores CJC, Rocío was often asked to question people or observe them, because of her skill at reading people. She wasn't often asked by other districts to do so.

Isis, of course, asked the question outright even though she had no official right. "What expertise is that?"

"It looks like there might be trouble. There's a crowd on the docks, shouting about foreigners," the chaski said. She looked scared and a little excited, and though she looked old for a chaski, on the verge of graduating, she was still young enough that danger was titillating.

The word "foreigners" tightened the stubborn knot of worry that hadn't left Rocío's stomach in three months.

"Hm." Hala tapped her lips slowly with two steepled fingers. "What else did she say?"

"Well..." The chaski looked around the office, her gaze coming back to Isis. "I don't know I should say. She's not an advocate, is she?"

"Excellent observation skills," Isis said. "I'll be on my way." She poked Rocío in the shoulder. "I'm not done talking to you. Bye, Hala." She put on her sun hat, a deceptively simple affair embroidered with red and blue flowers that cost more than the chaski's entire outfit.

"You and I are never done talking, Isis, dear," Rocío said lightly now that she had a reprieve in sight.

After she left, the chaski lowered her voice to almost a whisper and leaned in close to Hala. "The crowd is saying the river folk brought MMFs to the city."

Paco made an unhappy sound deep in his throat. His leg had been broken by a mob when MMFs were literally flying overhead and people had panicked trying to get away.

Rocío squeezed his shoulder, the motion keeping her from rubbing the bite scars on her hands. The tension in her stomach ratcheted up another notch. There was no way there were MMFs in the city again. Rocío and Hala had caught the man responsible, Hector Collins, and after one of the quickest adjudications in the history of the city, he'd been transported to the Ka Empire to the south. Surely no one else was both disturbed and skilled enough to copy him. He'd been a doctor, trained in his native magic to manipulate the domesticated fairies in his home country of Enkladt and had imported a limited supply. Magic expired in a matter of days outside its geographic origin, which was why there were no electric lights or appliances outside La Bene. Only the ocean trip had delayed that process, but the MMFs were doomed from the moment they landed.

Importing MMFs overland from the north was ridiculous. Surely river travel didn't have the same preserving effect.

"You see why she wants your help," the chaski said. "Will you come to *The Resolute*? That's a boat."

Hala stood abruptly, sending her chair screeching across the tiles behind her. "We've heard that name before." She loaded her pockets with what she considered essential equipment.

"The river woman was buying quinine." Rocío gulped the last of her tea and hooked her baton onto her shorts, though she disliked it. She preferred to talk her way out of things whenever possible.

"We should bring a chaski." Hala didn't look up from rummaging in her desk.

"Yup." Rocío scanned the room. Paco met her eyes and then looked away unhappily. The brace kept him at the CJC. "It's coming off soon," she said, knowing it probably felt like an eternity to him. "And there's plenty for you to do here. Go find the desk advocate and tell them to be ready just in case."

Just then Khadija bounced into the room, her glossy black hair coiled so tightly to her head not even a wisp escaped. She couldn't be more different than the Sanblas chaski: a few years younger, hawk nosed, dark skinned and with a serious case of hero worship of Hala.

Rocío changed her "Perfect" to "Khadija, we need you," out of consideration for Paco, and sent her to get her things.

CHAPTER 3

Rocío HEARD the trouble before she saw it. Angry voices rumbled through the air, and the sharp crack of wood hitting wood made the Sanblas chaski flinch. They hurried their steps, rounding the corner of a warehouse and came upon the Río ja' mayu. The far bank was hazy with distance and the humid air. This far north of the sea, the river was placid, only a few ripples in the water betraying the deeper currents, its deep brown-purple color due to the heavy load of silt it carried hundreds of kilometers from the mountains.

If Rocío looked downriver, to her left, she could see the masts of the seagoing vessels and the cranes to unload them cluttering the skyline, and hear the faint shouts of workers and the thud of cargo hitting wooden decks. The docks directly in front of her were reserved for the boats that came down from the agricultural outposts of the Ya Empire, where the river folk took on fruit and vegetables and sold them in La Bene.

By some accident of timing, only one berth was occupied. The boat and dock should have seethed with Benerex and river folk alike unloading cargo as fast as possible, with someone from the customs house checking the manifest. Instead the crane stood immobile, and about thirty people, all Benerex, gathered on the land side of the dock, with one nervous-looking advocate on the border between cobblestones and wooden pier.

The advocate had the shortest haircut Rocío had ever seen, on anyone. Hala's hair was short and not fashionable, but she managed to make it look good. This woman's scalp shone white through the bristles of her black hair, like she had been shaved for lice, and not gently at that.

She was also young enough that she had probably only just received her promotion to advocate. What had her chief been thinking, letting her out alone? Sanblas was already a rough neighborhood, with its sailors, dockworkers, bars and gambling dens; add in the river folk, who were notoriously suspicious of outsiders and a green advocate and you had a script for disaster. Rocío wasn't sure what was holding the crowd in check.

"Silvia Dante Ruíz, you arrest these people right now," a woman shouted.

"Aunt Pipina, you know I can't do that," the advocate said reasonably, with the tone of someone who'd repeated variations throughout the years.

Familial relationships. That accounts for the unexpected restraint of the crowd.

"You arrest them or we'll kill them. Monsters! My children work here," a man yelled.

The aunt turned on him, grabbed his shirt sleeve and started haranguing him.

The advocate spotted Rocío and Hala and waved them forward. A few people in the crowd turned to look but most didn't move.

"Excuse me," Hala said politely if loudly to the wall of backs.

Silvia called, "My experts are here now, you can go home. We'll take care of it."

The woman closest to Rocío wheeled, glaring and unwelcoming.

"Señorx Soledad," Rocío said, recognizing the owner of a nearby tavern. Unfortunately she was the only familiar face and she didn't like anyone. People went to her tavern for her chicha and grilled octopus, not for her personality. But Rocío had worked with less. "You know it'll be easier for us to resolve this problem without a crowd of angry Benerex making the river folk feel trapped."

"You can't fix this so easily," Señorx Soledad said, shaking a wooden spoon at Rocío. "They're hiding a foreign magicker who's got those MMFs, we're not leaving until we know it's safe."

Rocío was only able to suppress her flinch because of the chaski's warning. Crowd control was all about finding a solution people would agree to and keeping everyone calm, and the advocates had to look calmer than everyone else to get there. Rocío eyed the spoon and pushed it aside with two fingers.

Señorx Soledad had the grace to look slightly abashed and lowered it. "I was cooking when my nephew told me."

The Sanblas chaski had slipped into the crowd and was talking urgently to a man with a loading hook in his hand. More people stopped yelling and turned to look at the newcomers.

"If it's true, you've done your job of notifying the authorities," Rocío tapped herself on her chest, "and you'd do better making sure your tavern isn't burning down because your cooking oil is unattended on your stove."

"And we don't know that it's true at all. All we know is that someone is sick. People get sick," the young advocate said a little desperately.

Rocío gestured for Silvia to stop speaking, but the other advocate missed it.

"Let's not jump to conclusions. I can't find out what's going on because I'm here arguing with you," Silvia said.

"Why don't you jump in the river?" a man shouted.

"You don't talk to my niece like that." Aunt Pipina rounded on him.

"Would I be standing right here, if I really thought there were MMFs flying around?" Silvia shouted back, her voice cracking with overuse.

"You're paid to take that kind of risk," a different man said.

Hala drew Khadija behind her protectively. "Are you sure *you* should be standing here, if you truly believe there are MMFs?" Hala said to him. "Following your logic, the only safe course of action is for you to leave so we can attend to the situation."

"Those things could be anywhere by now," another man said, squinting at the sky, hunching his shoulders.

Rocío reflexively scanned the sky too, remembered anxiety wringing her stomach. *I really hope not.*

"She's right," someone else muttered.

"If it's MMFs, and that's a big if, we need to move quickly," Rocío said. "I know. You know that too." She made a quick gesture that displayed the scars on her hands.

Señorx Soledad tested one of the scars with a thick callused finger. Rocío barely felt it through the scar tissue. Expression moved over Señorx Soledad's face like a wave. "Let them through," she said, and a path opened up, some people moving more grudgingly than others.

"Thank you, Señorx," Hala said. She glanced at Rocío, communicating her unwillingness to separate in a potential mob.

"Do you want to stay here?" Rocío asked the Sanblas chaski, who was still hanging onto the man with the loading hook. He looked like he might be her uncle or cousin.

"Why? Are you trying to protect me?"

"I was thinking you could talk to them, keep them calm, maybe get them to leave?"

"How should I do that?" She squinted suspiciously at Rocío, the expression incongruous on her baby face. "I'm not an advocate."

Rocío shaped her answer carefully, aware of the crowd listening. "You're something even better: familiar and young, therefore not threatening. Just talk to them. Ask about their concerns—that's something you should be doing as part of your training. That'll give them two things they'll like—airing their grievances and helping someone. Really. Ask them things they know the answers to. People love sharing their expertise."

Señorx Soledad snorted.

"So true," Hala muttered.

Rocío elbowed her gently in the side. "You would know. It's up to you," she said more quietly to the chaski. "Do you think your presence will calm them or make them more protective and angry? You know a lot of them, right?"

The girl took the time to think about it. "Okay. I'll"—she changed what she was going to say at some hidden signal from her relative—"we'll try to keep them calm."

"Good enough." It was a sign of how strange life had gotten that she thought it was safer to leave a chaski with a potential mob than risk MMFs. She leveled a considering gaze at Khadija.

"No way," Khadija said, her chin jutting out stubbornly.

Rocío sighed but gave in, and they joined Silvia on the other side of the invisible line.

"Please stay there," Silvia urged the crowd before leading Rocío, Hala and Khadija down the length of the dock. The crowd stayed on the cobblestones, as if keeping their feet on land in the city provided some kind of protection.

Rocío kept an eye on Khadija. The girl's eyes were wide and her lips a bit tense, but she moved easily and didn't seem cowed or too scared. The smell of fish and sea wrack was stronger here, layered over with the incongruous smell of cooking peaches.

"I'm Silvia Dante Ruíz. Thank you for coming." She shook their hands. Her grip was a little too damp and firm, hanging onto Rocío's like she was one of the orange life savers hanging on the boat's railings.

"Of course we came," Rocío said, injecting warmth into her voice. "Advocates help advocates. You did a good job with that crowd." Later she'd find out why this young advocate was here alone, without a partner or other support from her CJC.

Silvia laughed nervously and tugged at her long sleeves. "I didn't do anything."

"They didn't throw you into the river and they didn't rush you," Rocío pointed out.

"Oh, that's just because some of them know me."

"One of the founding principles of community justice," Hala said. "So what do you know?"

"About as much you do, now. Rumors that these river folk are sick, which quickly became rumors that they were sick because they had brought MMFs to the city. I was with a safety inspector, writing tickets for violations in the warehouse over there when we heard the commotion."

Rocío turned her attention to the boat while Silvia talked. At this end of the dock, the somnolence of the warm summer afternoon reasserted itself, an impression heightened by the lack of visible people on board. The boat creaked with the river current, rubbing against its moorings. It was long and wide, with a shallow draft and an open deck packed tight with crates and bundles. She vaguely remembered that the three-story wooden building in the stern was called a pilot house and that it contained the steering mechanism, the boilers for the paddle wheel and housing for the crew. She was more certain that the blue pennant with five white stars identified it as belonging to river folk. Water slapped softly against the hull, and ducks quacked as they paddled by. The discussion at the end of the dock was softened by distance and, Rocío hoped, compassion.

"The crew wouldn't let me on when I asked and I didn't want to try to force the issue by myself. The safety inspector went to Sanblas to get help. I don't know why no one has come yet, unless everyone is still meeting with the harbormaster about black market cacao beans."

That was a shame. The chief of the Sanblas CJC was a no-nonsense former sailor who could have straight talked the crowd into leaving with a few promises of drinks and updates. Silvia was too young and uncertain to exert the same effect, and Hala and Rocío were too much the outsiders.

Silvia raised a hand to hair and then lowered it without touching her almost-bare scalp. A look of dismay crossed her face and disappeared. "The first mate said it's just regular sickness, not even malaria, and told me to go away. But when she came on deck, the dockworkers and neighbors and local businesspeople acted up and everything sort of escalated. It seemed like it was better for her to stay out of sight. I thought you could tell everyone it's not MMFs and get them to go away." Her gaze bounced anxiously between Hala's and Rocío's faces.

"I would have done the same," Rocío said, and Silvia's face relaxed.

"I'll call her? The first mate?" She raised her voice. "Ahoy, *The*

Resolute. I brought more advocates to talk to you, Pilar. Can we come aboard?"

Rocío heard the name of the river woman from the summer market without surprise. Hala folded her arms and leaned on one of the piles.

For a moment there was no movement on the boat. Then one person strolled out from between the crates, and then another, until about ten people lined the rail, arms crossed, or feet spread wide, an aggressive wall of unwelcome. They were dressed like Pilar had been in the market: a loose brown or bronze sarong separated into trousers by a sash between the legs, bare chested or with brief bright vests and braided hair. Their hard gazes strayed between the advocates in front of them and the cluster of people at the end of the dock. None of them spoke.

The deck-level door of the building opened wider and a woman's voice floated out. "No. Go away."

Silvia glanced pleadingly at Rocío, who gestured for her to continue. Rocío needed to know about Silvia, and letting her talk was one way to evaluate what the young advocate was like.

"Señorx Pilar, we need to talk about this," Silvia said. "It will reassure the people here that the rumors aren't true if you let us come aboard."

"So you can beat us up?"

"I would never do that, Señorx Pilar! I uphold the law."

"Why should we believe you?"

"Because the CJC serves everyone in La Bene, river folk and dockworkers alike."

"That's what you say, but no will notice if a few river folk disappear into your prisons."

One of the crew members grumbled something and smacked the shaft of his cargo hook into his palm. Aside from his clothing and hair, he could have been a twin to the chaski's relative with his muscles and uncompromising expression.

Silvia wiped sweat off her forehead, avoiding contact with her hair. "We don't have prisons."

"Forced labor, then and transportation."

"Señorx Pilar, I brought you experts. If you're telling the truth, they'll know. They were there—right there—when the real MMFs were let loose." She turned a beseeching look on Hala.

"You're doing fine," Hala said. She didn't say *For a very inexperienced advocate*, but Rocío knew she was thinking it.

The boat creaked. A seagull flapped to the dock and regarded them with one alien eye. Rocío slapped at a tickle on her bare arm and smashed a gnat. Not anything worse. Not a mosquito of any kind. "I think we've met, Señorx Pilar," Rocío called finally, judging Silvia was at the end of her ability. "Why don't you come out and see?"

The woman from the summer market appeared in the open doorway and shaded her eyes from the sun. "You?" She stepped out. Dark patches stained her vest and new lines drew the features of her face down in exhaustion. Her braids were coming undone, and locks of hair clung to her neck.

"Hello, again, Pilar of *The Resolute*. You remember, I'm Detective Haddad and this is Detective Díaz. We'd like to help." Hala held up a small change purse and shook it, setting the coins jingling. "You missed the adjudication, but it was in your favor even without your testimony. We have your change from the chemist. The chemist is doing community service work."

Silvia gaped at Hala.

"Coincidence," Rocío told her. She raised her voice. "She also has to donate medication equal to the value she tried to steal from you."

Pilar swayed, counter to the motion of the boat and wiped her forehead with the back of her hand.

Hala let the silence stretch. Silvia made to speak and Rocío stopped her with a raised hand.

The crew's stares were no less hostile.

"No," Pilar said tiredly, bracing her hands on the doorframe as if to physically bar them when they came. As she must know they would.

"Señorx Pilar..." Silvia trailed off.

After so many years working together Hala's glance at Rocío was enough to assign their roles. Hala would do the hard talking. Rocío would be sympathetic.

"Señorx Pilar of *The Resolute*, we have been notified of sickness aboard. By the law of La Bene, advocates have the right to enter any home or dwelling to pursue a matter of public health. Your trade here is predicated on your adherence to our law. I can have the harbormaster secure your boat, even bar you from our port."

There were plenty of small cities inside the Ya Empire, but the money was made trading between them and La Bene. Being barred from La Bene's port wouldn't wholly impoverish them, but their standard of living, probably already balanced on a razor edge, would become even more precarious, especially after this trip. They should have left with their cargo days ago.

For the first time Rocío saw doubt in the glances of the crew and the shuffling of their feet. "Let us on board, Pilar. There are too many angry people on both sides."

Pilar sagged. With a glance, she seemed to consult one of the crew, an older, sinewy woman, and then nodded once, briefly. "You stay there," she told her crew.

Hala climbed aboard first, her heels thumping hollowly on the deck. Rocío and Silvia followed less noisily and Khadija, last, was soundless. They entered the cramped quarters, a series of small rooms parallel to the boxy stern. At a glance from Hala, Khadija hung back, just barely inside the first doorway.

Rocío looked around curiously. She had never been on a river boat before. A man sprawled unconscious in a hammock in one corner, Pilar blocking him from sight with her hands on her hips. Two kids, aged about four and six, huddled in another in spite of the sweat plastering their hair to their foreheads and necks. More hammocks were bundled against the walls out of the way and cabinets lined another wall. In spite of the painfully clean floorboards and the wide open window that let in light, the room smelled of sick sweat and vomit. Rocío didn't know if the starkness spoke of poverty or the strict discipline of a living space that moved beneath the owners' feet.

Pilar watched them narrowly as they filled up her bare, little home. Her chin trembled, and then she spoke, quickly and roughly. "It's a lie, what they're saying." She jerked her chin in the direction of land. "It wasn't us. We wouldn't—can't—do that dirty magic." She backed up stiffly until she bumped into the wall next to the sick man's hammock, revealing the red bite marks on his hands and arms, as big as the nail on her pinky finger. They looked like MMF bites.

Rocío shuddered. If the dockworkers had seen this, the boat would already be burning to the waterline.

Rocío hadn't run screaming in November when the MMFs had converged in an angry cloud around her, and she wouldn't bolt now, but for a moment the urge, surging out of the past, almost overwhelmed her. So many had died. She sucked in a breath, steadying herself. *These people are alive and need our help. Or they need to be stopped from hurting others.*

Khadija made a pained noise deep in her throat. Rocío put a comforting hand on her shoulder and immediately felt more in control of herself.

"May I examine him?" Hala asked, courteously waiting for Pilar's head jerk before moving forward.

The man was older than Pilar and similar to her in coloring: light brown hair and dark skin, the hook in his nose more pronounced, and the same small ears. Hala pulled on gloves from one the many pockets in her broadcloth trousers before testing his temperature with a hand against his forehead. "What's his name?"

"Costas."

He didn't respond to his name and seemed unaware they were in the room.

Frowning, Hala pinched the skin on the back of his hand. With a tailor's tape she measured the bite marks on his hands and then laid her arm next to his to compare her scars through a magnifying glass she extracted from another of her pockets.

"You brought a magnifying glass?" Silvia asked uncertainly.

Rocío grinned a little harder than she usually would to try to ease the tension. "On slow days we bet on what she doesn't have in her pockets."

"Did he say anything about being bitten?" Hala asked.

"We found him like this, unconscious, four days ago. He hasn't woken up."

"Found him?" Hala asked. "Where?"

"At the foot of the gangway."

Hala nodded absently, still examining the bite marks. "They're the right size. The scabbing indicates that they are more than a day old, but not more than four." She turned to Pilar. "Did he have these bites before he left the boat?"

Pilar hugged her arms around herself. "I swear he didn't. He would have said. But who is going to believe me?"

"Why can't you tell me from your own observations?"

Pilar unfastened one of the cabinets, jerked it open and picked out a leather arm bracer tooled with viridian quetzal birds. "He wears these all the time."

"Including the night you found him?" Hala put out her hand and Pilar gave her the bracer. Held against Costas's arm, it was obvious it would have covered the skin where most of the bites clustered.

"Yes," Pilar said defiantly.

Hala handed it back. Pilar clutched it to her chest before replacing it and then moved to stand between the advocates and the children. The little girl curled her fingers in the edge of Pilar's shirt, and Pilar covered her fingers with her own.

"Were you or the children bitten? No? Anyone else on the crew? Did you see anything that could be responsible for these marks?"

Pilar shook her head.

"Do you have fleas? Bedbugs?"

"We're not dirty savages," Pilar bit out.

"It's difficult to get rid of the vermin once infested. They're a common problem in La Bene as well. I'm attempting to rule out other possible causes for the bites. The scabbing makes them difficult to identify."

Pilar glared at her. "We fumigate, just like rich city people."

"Do you know how these rumors started about MMFs?"

Pilar shook her head, her lips pressed so tightly together they almost disappeared.

"What about you, Silvia? Do you know how the rumors started?" Hala pocketed the magnifying glass and stripped off her gloves, turning them inside out.

Silvia shifted uncomfortably. "I didn't ask, and everyone was too busy yelling at me to tell me anything useful. I thought they might get more agitated and rush the boat if I brought it up."

"You made the right choice, prioritizing the safety of the river folk," Rocío said. She would have patted Silvia's shoulder like she had Khadija's but the tilt of Silvia's chin warned her off.

"I thought you would be able to help," Silvia burst out. "Everyone knows what you did. That you identified the foreign—the man behind the MMFs."

Hala's mouth turned down but she ignored Silvia's slip. "Costas is dangerously dehydrated—"

"I've been giving him water!" Pilar's voice shook.

"I have no doubt you are, however he's not able to swallow enough in this state. He needs to go to the Hospital."

Pilar shook her head, her expression despairing.

"And the illness...?" Silvia said. "Is it...?"

"A doctor needs to make that determination," Hala said.

"You can see why he needs a doctor, don't you, Señorx Pilar?" Rocío asked. "Can I talk to your children?"

"Why?"

"To make sure they're feeling okay."

Pilar glared at her but bent to whisper to her children, her body language softening. Rocío couldn't quite hear, but it didn't look like she was telling the children to lie; she looked like a mother at the end of her rope.

"They're not sick. Just scared."

"I would be, too." Rocío decided to take that as permission and crouched to be on eye level with the kids. "Hi. My name is Chío. Does your mom let you chew gum?" She showed the package to Pilar, who nodded warily. "Your mom says it's okay." Rocío took out two pieces.

The boy, who was older, took them, turning them over in his hands and looking a question at his mother. She nodded again, and he unwrapped one for his sister and put the second piece in the front pocket of his shirt.

"Don't swallow it," Rocío reminded her. "How about you? Are you feeling okay?"

"We're not sick," the boy said. The girl stared at Rocío with huge eyes.

"Did you see what happened to your uncle?"

The boy shook his head. The girl hid her face in his shoulder.

Pilar moved in front of them. "That's enough."

Rocío pushed to her feet, her knees clicking.

"I can't take him to the Hospital," Pilar said. "The people out there would sooner kill us than let us by."

Silvia rubbed her mouth, looking like she agreed. Khadija watched wide-eyed, her lips moving as if she were memorizing everything she observed.

"You have a dingy," Rocío said. "You can row down the river. It's closer to the Hospital anyway."

Pilar shook her head in stubborn refusal.

"Señorx Pilar, I'm sure you know people can die of dehydration even without a complicating illness. The doctors here have the experience your brother needs. He probably won't survive without their care," Hala said. "In this heat, the dehydration is only going to get worse. The doctors know how to treat it."

Pilar pinched her lips together and brushed sweaty hair off the boy's forehead. "Okay," she said, almost voicelessly, after another minute. "I'll talk to my crew." She herded the children out the door.

Silvia made to follow but Rocío waved her to stay.

"What do you think?" Rocío asked Hala.

"The only way there could be MMFs in the city again is if someone brought them."

"This kind of boat can't go in the ocean, if that helps," Silvia said. "It couldn't navigate and might even be torn apart by the stress of the waves and the currents."

"Which would rule out the river folk," Hala frowned, clearly running something through her mind.

"And yet..." Rocío said.

"And yet," Hala agreed. "We cannot take the chance that someone has found a way to replicate the threat. We need to search the boat. We can't risk assumptions."

"Is it possible she's an innocent victim?" Silvia asked.

"It's too early to eliminate any possibilities," Hala said, "including that she is innocent or a victim."

Rocío evaluated Silvia again. "How do you feel about accompanying Pilar to the Hospital on your own?"

"You mean if they try to pitch me overboard?" She drew herself up straighter. "I can handle myself. And I can swim if I have to," she added in a more reflective tone.

CHAPTER 4

THE NEXT HALF hour was consumed with transferring Costas to a dingy with the help of the two brothers, Sujay and Victor, who were going to accompany Costas, Pilar and the children. Lowering the unconscious man into the dingy was a difficult task, exacerbated by the crew's efforts to not draw the attention of the crowd that still stood at the end of the dock, in defiance of all sorts of common sense and the heat. In contrast, Pilar's kids scrambled down with the agility of extreme youth and eagerness to get away. They settled confidently next to Sanjay, the bearded older brother.

Rocío squinted, trying to estimate whether there were more or fewer agitators than before. As one of the crew members settled the oars in the locks, he hit it sharply against the hull.

One of the people on land yelled out, "They're getting away!"

Of course the loudest mouth among them had to yell something inflammatory and not innocuous.

Someone cursed loudly and a few people yelled indistinctly. The crowd heaved as individuals went in separate directions, trying to see what was happening. A few crowded too close to the edge of the river.

Rocío shouted, "Be careful!" But it was too late. A girl with wispy brown hair windmilled frantically, tipped and hit the water with a large splash. She disappeared under the surface.

"Girl overboard!" A man bellowed.

"That was the Sanblas chaski," Rocío said. "She must be able to swim..."

Khadija strained forward over the railing searching for a sign of her.

A man dived in, cutting the water with barely a splash. A woman followed.

The chaski surfaced some distance away, gasping and flailing, and then disappeared under the surface again. The male rescuer dived again, and the woman struck out towards where the chaski had been.

Rocío held her breath. As if that would help. Long minutes seemed to pass. The second rescuer treaded water, scanning the surface. Something caught her attention and she stroked forward a meter.

The water churned and the first diver surfaced. A second later he pulled the girl's face up. The woman pounded on the chaski's back and she coughed, instinctively curling forward into the water again until her rescuers forced her head back.

"She's okay!" The man yelled.

Rocío could see the tension run out of the crowd. She turned, looking for the dingy, but it had rowed out of sight, aided by the ebbing tide, while the drama had played out on the docks. "They're gone," Rocío told Hala.

"Hm. Interesting."

The rescuers handed the chaski up to the dock. She sat, head drooping, legs hanging over the water, while several people milled around her. The crisis seemed to break the group's cohesion. A few people peeled off, looking like they had errands to run, and a few more wandered away. They might even disperse now, without that critical mass that made individuals into the many-headed beast with one mind — a mob.

Rocío turned her attention back to the boat and the remaining crew. They bunched together, legs braced apart, arms folded across their chests or fingers flexed as they gripped their hips with elbows flared. So: feeling attacked, ready to fight or flee, suspicious and belligerent. Not unusual in these types of situations, though this situation was a tad unusual.

Rocío had a patter for this and an empathetic tone that was as important as the words. Hala observed without drawing attention to herself.

"We're here to help," Rocío began. "I know it's hard for you to believe that, but Costas is very sick and he needs more help than you can give him right now." This was a large boat, but a small community. It would be hard to keep a secret, if Pilar had even tried. Costas was their captain after all, and they'd been stuck, idle, at port for days now. How much did they know or suspect? It was too early for Rocío to ask; they wouldn't answer and that would set a pattern of behavior it would be hard to break. So, frank disclosure.

"Pilar thinks your captain has been bitten by MMFs."

They exchanged unhappy glances, but no one looked surprised.

She showed them the backs of her hands, fingers spread, so they could see the scars. Months later, the angry red was finally fading and some were pale and gray, while others were puckered and raised but closer to her normal light brown skin tone. "I know exactly what that's like. He's going to get the same care I did when I was bitten by MMFs." Rocío could keep talking forever, trying to put them at ease, but the urgency of the situation gnawed at her. "I survived. There's no reason your captain can't survive, too."

They were softening. Fingers not so tense, shoulders lowered. That had to be enough. "We need you to help us help him. His health is out of our hands, out of your hands, but anything you tell us, something you know, could help us figure out what has truly happened. We're not sure it is MMFs but can't ignore the possibility. If it is, we need to stop anyone else from being infected." She swallowed, her throat suddenly dry as the reality of the situation hit her again. She pushed it down. She couldn't afford to be scared or upset. "Right now we're all at risk if there are MMFs loose in the city again." She didn't want to mention their children, that might sound like a threat. "I have a niece and nephew that I want to protect." That did it. A few faces softened, and one woman's chin shook as if she had swallowed down tears. "You can help me by answering our questions."

She decided she needed to break the tension more before bringing up the next topic. "Who is in charge with the captain and

Pilar—she's the first mate, yes? With both of them away?" Rocío looked away from the woman she'd pegged and pointed to the least likely looking one; he had a thin beard and skin pebbled with the acne of youth. "Is it you?"

Half of them took it as a joke; the sinewy woman who Rocío had identified as the next in charge stepped forward, asserting her authority. She was older than Pilar and Costas combined, with gray hair sticking straight out like a dandelion.

"I'm the second mate. Are you going to search our boat?" she asked in a voice raspy from shouting.

"Why do you ask?"

"It's what your sort always do. We don't have anything to hide, but you don't go anywhere without one of us watching you."

"Sounds fair," Rocío said cheerfully, having achieved exactly what she wanted; now she didn't have to be the one to bring up the subject of a search. "We know it's your home and we'll be respectful. Who do you want to go with Hala while she gets started with the cargo?"

Rocío didn't catch whatever signals passed among the crew, but a lanky young woman with veins standing out over her well-defined muscles peeled out of the group.

"I apologize in advance for looking through your living quarters. Are you with me?" Rocío asked the second mate.

She nodded once.

Interesting choice. The assignments seemed to indicate the second mate wasn't concerned about the cargo but was concerned about Rocío's questions. That could be for a variety of reasons, from the fact that they had nothing to hide to a belief that their hiding spaces were well concealed. Hala had excellent spatial skills, so Rocío had no worries about the crew getting away with anything of the sort.

Hala rolled a set of dice on top of the nearest crate. She counted down the rows and pointed to fifth crate in the second row said, "Could you open that one please?"

"What are the dice for?" the young crew woman asked.

Hala's explanation about the impossibility of choosing randomly without a tool of some kind faded as they worked their way down the narrow aisle between the cargo, Khadija trailing behind.

Rocío got the second mate to warm up to won't-leave-ice-burns level by asking how many people were on board and whether they were entirely a family group or not. She learned that there were thirty, including kids, all related by blood or marriage; Costas and Pilar and the woman with Hala were siblings; the rest were cousins and aunts and uncles and spouses. Pilar didn't currently have a spouse. She had been married short term to a Benerex and the children had stayed with her as part of that contract. Costas's spouses and some of the other adults had taken the children sightseeing in the city to distract them when it became clear how sick the captain was.

"Why didn't Pilar's children go with the others?"

The second mate, whose name was Buenaventura, spit tobacco over the rail and shrugged. "Over protective."

Rocío switched to asking about the voyage. It took the river folk somewhere in the neighborhood of four days to travel down the river from the nearest town in the Ya Empire. They had arrived on 29 January, too late to unload. The same night Costas got sick. That meant if he'd been bitten by MMFs, it had been the same day, in La Bene, or the day before, just outside La Bene.

On the thirtieth, the crew had transferred their cargo, produce from the Ya Empire: winter corn, winter squash, okra, onions, beets and cabbage. On the thirty-first, they had taken on their return cargo: smoked fish and pork, dried seaweed, sand, salt, preserved lemons, and raisins. Once it was clear the peaches and plums would rot in the hold while they waited for the captain to recover, they had made preserves. That explained the cooked peaches smell that still hung around the boat.

"Normal times, we'd leave that night or the next morning at the latest. Couldn't this time. Because of the captain."

The crew hid the fear from their faces, but Rocío saw it in their sidelong glances, clenched hands and shuffling feet. "We have good doctors here in La Bene. They'll do everything they can to save him. They saved me and my partner." She displayed the scars on her hands again.

This time a young man leaned forward to look, his Adam's apple bobbing.

"If they bother," someone in the back muttered.

He flinched back.

"They will," Rocío said firmly. "Did you stop anywhere just outside of La Bene? Do you travel at night?"

"We tie up at night," Buenaventura said. "At markers."

"What does that mean?" Rocío asked.

The second mate sighed and jerked her head, indicating Rocío should follow. Instead of taking the stairs to the pilot house, as Rocío half expected, Buenaventura led the way back to the living quarters. Rocío detoured to lean over the railing to check the crowd on the docks. Still there, but much reduced. A few sat on the ground now with shirts draped over their heads. Hot out there, with no shade.

Inside, the second mate plucked a rolled chart and a thick oblong book from a shelf. "Captain's log. I'll want that back."

"Isn't this usually up in the pilot house?"

"Pilar was updating it."

Buenaventura unrolled the chart and placed her thumb over a square labeled "Three." "That's where we spent the last night outside La Bene."

"How far out of the city is that?"

"Just under seventy kilometers."

Rocío turned her attention to the log. The soft leather cover was water stained, the black ink denoting the date bleeding into the brown leather. She flipped through, catching glimpses of different handwriting, a sketch of a pod of river dolphins in grays and pinks that had exactly captured their joie de vivre, and a meticulously labeled drawing of a flower she didn't recognize, some kind of yellow and orange orchid. More information than she could skim quickly.

She closed it and tucked it under her arm. "I'll need to go through this. You'll get it back." If she spent much longer with the second mate, she'd be speaking in monosyllables too. Not that she blamed the woman for being wary, prejudice being what it was in the city. It was easy for Benerex to blame itinerants for theft and sickness when they weren't around to speak up for themselves, even though La Bene was a city built of refugees and immigrants.

Rocío made a quick search of the rooms, taking in details she hadn't noticed before. The normal possessions of thirty adults and children living on a boat: clothes, keepsakes ranging from a shiny piece of rock to old-fashioned miniature portraits in tooled gold cases, three packs of cards, bows and arrows and a hunting rifle, and some jewelry in cheap metals with glass stones but careful craftsmanship. On one side of an inner room, an altar was bolted to the wall, portraits surrounding it, a visual history of family and ancestors. Rocío found a drawing in colored pencil of a man and a photograph of a smiling woman with a funerary card from Hidalgo y Ortega Cemetery tucked below the photo, dated a few years ago. Rocío thought they might be Pilar's parents. The flower offerings, purple water hyacinths, were wilting in the heat and the usual candles were missing, but that seemed common sense on a boat.

At Rocío's gesture, the second mate unlocked a small chest, revealing papers and a soft purse. Rocío made sure the second mate could see what she did as she twisted the catch. It held a jumble of currencies, from Benerex pesos to Ya zals and Ka sols. Rocío shook it idly and stopped abruptly. A few Enkladt pennies had sifted to the surface.

It was unusual to see Enkladt money. The small country was far across the ocean, practically on the other side of the world, and had very little that La Bene couldn't get much closer to hand. But here and now, it was ominous. The inventor of the MMFs was from Enkladt.

Of course the river folk were traders and all sorts of coins passed through their hands as well as goods.

Rocío opened her mouth to question Buenaventura when Hala's piercing wolf whistle cut the air.

Rocío snapped the purse closed and dashed out onto the deck. Shading her eyes, she turned in a slow circle searching for her partner. The crew were sitting or leaning on crates staring at the pilothouse behind and above Rocío. Hala whistled again, more softly, and Rocío turned around and looked up.

Hala stood on the roof. Rocío knew her partner. Even three stories up she knew something was wrong from Hala's rigid spine.

Rocío raced to the narrow stairs on the port side and took them two at a time, Buenaventura treading on her heels.

The pilothouse was smaller than the lower two floors, almost like a house centered in a yard, except here it was a cabin surrounded with wooden planking. The open windows showed an empty room and a big steering wheel inside.

"Aft," Buenaventura said, leading Rocío to the rear. This side had two smaller windows on either side of a ladder. Eyes closed, Hala leaned against the wall, still rigid. Khadija clutched Hala's arm, half hidden behind her, gulping short shallow breaths.

Rocío throat closed up. A vision of Hala bitten again, sick again, made her sight go dark for a moment. "Hala!" she choked out.

"Don't—it's dead." Hala pointed up.

At the edge of the roof, the stained glass precision of mosquito wings as big as Rocío's palm glinted malevolently. She immediately recognized the elongated shape and pattern of veins. A grue slithered down her spine. So pretty for something so deadly. They had barely survived the first attack—there was no other word for the unleashing of a biological weapon.

Rocío sucked in another breath and held it, trying not to hyperventilate. *Think, pierdate.* She looked at Buenaventura.

Confusion. Buenaventura looked from Hala to the wings to Rocío. Her eyes widened. "Is that—" Her eyes narrowed and her nostrils flared with disgust. She stepped back. And again.

Rocío grabbed Buenaventura, stopping her before she backed right off the roof.

"Hala?"

"It is dead." Hala opened her eyes. They reflected the bleakness in Rocío's own heart. She had thought they were done with this. Hala blanked her expression and turned to Khadija, murmuring something reassuring.

Rocío forced herself to take slower, controlled breaths, combatting the adrenaline that was narrowing her vision and making her heart pound. She shoved the purse into her pocket and passed the captain's log to Khadija. The girl fumbled it and then pressed it to her chest. The wooden ladder was smooth under Rocío's hands, well-cared for. The sun was hot on her scalp. A bird called.

As she climbed, she became aware that the wings could not be attached to a body—they were jammed in a seam between two shingles. Another step. Her head rose above the level of the roof and her hands tightened on the final rung.

Almost in the middle of the flat roof lay a tiny, motionless body. Its mosquito wings, if the mosquito were the size of a swallow, spread limply to either side, framing a naked, human-shaped body with light-colored skin turned pasty and waxy with death. The body was so perfectly formed it was disturbing. The tiny toes. The perfect little fingernails. And then that face. Sharp. Malevolent. Twisted. Hungry.

"Is there another one?" Hala asked. "To go with the wings?" It was a measure of how shaken she was that she asked. There was only one dead fairy thing up here, that was obvious. "Last time," Hala's words slowed as if she was internally checking the validity of a next time—now time—"we found them whole. Not de-winged. Or disembodied."

Rocío laid her cheek against the shingles, sighting on the detached wings. "No blood. I suppose they could have gotten jammed in here by themselves...Hala, what do you think?" She wanted her partner back. If Hala was falling apart, there was little chance Rocío was going to hold it together. *No*, she thought with resolve, *I will hold it together for both of us.* It was a truism that people could manage incredible feats when they did it for other people. *I can handle one dead MMF.* It was everything it represented that was the problem.

The wings trembled and Rocío shuddered in response. "Are you sure it's dead?"

"It is," Hala said flatly.

The vibrations of the water against the hull then, magnified by the height of the pilothouse, giving it the semblance of life.

Rocío dropped down the ladder and leaned against it, much like Hala had. For a few moments, everyone was silent. Rocío at least was trying to master her emotions and not run screaming off the boat. That wouldn't help anyone.

"I don't like it," Hala said, her factual dry tone restored, a bulwark against terror.

"You don't like it?" Rocío squawked. "I don't expect you to like it! That's probably the most inane thing you've ever said."

"I am experiencing my own emotional reaction to the situation, Rocío," Hala said tartly.

Rocío breathed deeply, let the terror flow past her like a bore tide, imagining herself the indifferent rock cliff that withstood a million tides. "Right. Sorry. Right." Rocío patted Hala's shoulder as much for her own comfort as for Hala's. "I would never try to stop someone from experiencing their emotions."

Hala huffed a laugh, acknowledging the truth of that as well as the deeper truth, that it was one of Rocío's hard-won life maxims. In retrospect, Rocío's years on the stage before becoming a detective had probably been a form of self therapy.

"Khadija, are you okay?"

Khadija shuffled out from behind Hala. "I am," she said firmly.

"It's dead? You sure?" Buenaventura asked, in control of herself again.

You'd have to be made of stern stuff to crew a boat, I suppose, traveling through uninhabited or unfriendly territory with no one to depend on except each other.

"Very sure," Hala said. "I poked it with a pencil."

Rocío sucked in a sharp breath, but didn't scream at her partner for her foolhardiness. "We need to get it down. Hala, do you want to photograph it first?"

Hala gestured to her pants, her normal crispness returning. "I'm not carrying a camera. I believe speed is the better part of valor in this situation." She turned to the second mate. "Do you have a roll of paper or cloth we could insert under it? I'd prefer no one touch it."

Buenaventura was staring at the roof of the pilothouse, sucking on her stained teeth. "What? Oh, yes."

She turned to leave and Rocío blocked her with an arm. "You cannot talk about this."

"I'm going right in here." Buenaventura pointed to the pilothouse. "And I'm not saying a word. We have enough trouble already."

She returned quickly with a sheet of paper. Rocío could read enough Ya hieroglyphics to see that it was an old tariff announcement. "Gloves?" She didn't mean to touch the MMF if she could help it, but she'd have to touch the wings. Hala wordlessly offered a clean pair, relief in her eyes that Rocío was taking this task.

Back on the roof, Rocío tried to examine the MMF objectively as she maneuvered the paper under it. From head to toe, the fairy was less than twenty centimeters, the body narrow, with the wings extending maybe six centimeters on both sides for a total wingspan of sixteen centimeters. The wings were the easiest to look at, translucent, finely veined, rounded at the edges, because, besides their size, they were perfectly normal. The little humanoid body on the other hand...it gave her the creeps, like some of the puppets that were too close to lifelike while still being somehow wrong.

The body was slim and proportional, the hips narrow, the breasts almost non-existent. The face was twisted in a distorted sneer that reminded Rocío of some bitter bureaucrats entombed for life in the Office of Civil Statistics.

She folded the paper over the face and handed down the package to Hala, her hands sweating inside the gloves.

By the time she rejoined them on the lower roof, Hala was showing it to Buenaventura. The second mate pulled out a tin of chewing tobacco and and scooped a pinch into her mouth. "I've never seen that before," she grated out. "Get it off my boat."

Her own oral fixation activated, Rocío patted her pockets for gum and pulled out the captain's purse first. "Look at this." She gave it to Hala, found her gum and offered it around. Shrugging when no one else accepted, she folded a piece into her mouth. "Do you know where the Enkladt money is from?"

"What Enkladt money?" Buenaventura glared at her. When Hala held up one of the pennies, she barely glanced at it. "We're traders. There are coins from half a dozen countries in that purse at any one time."

Rocío stared at her hard. She might look like the muscle but she clearly was second mate for her brains as well, and shouldn't be underestimated. Rocío wished she had asked her next question before the MMF had disrupted their — not rapport, but at least cessation of outright hostilities. "Who inherits the boat if your captain dies?"

Buenaventura looked like she wanted to spit. Her lips pulled back in a sneer, revealing flecks of tobacco on her teeth, and the muscles in her arms stood out hard as rocks. "No one. The boat is owned by all of us."

"Ok, who becomes captain if he dies?"

"Pilar. But you landhuggers are more twisted than I thought if you believe she would kill her own brother so she can sit up late and do paperwork. We make decisions together. It's not like the Ya emperor in his headdress of quetzal feathers and jewels sitting on a throne."

That was quite a lot of cogent information from someone who looked like she wanted to punch them. Rocío could only assume Buenaventura was aware of just how bad this now looked for Pilar and was trying to control the situation as much as possible.

Hala tipped the coins back into the purse. "We need to talk to Pilar again. And see if Costas is conscious. Now."

"I'll get you something to put that in. The sooner you're off my boat the better." Buenaventura stomped down the stairs.

Now that they were alone, Rocío thought Khadija might accept a little comfort, not that she'd admit she needed it. "It's going to be all right," Rocío said, intentionally making her voice light for the teenager.

"You can't know that," Khadija said bleakly. "I thought we were done with the plague."

Hala put a hand on Khadija's shoulder and pressed down hard enough that the lines on her knuckles showed yellow against her dark skin. She said, "We know more this time. We're better prepared. It won't be like before." Khadija shuddered and sucked in a deep breath, some of the tension going out of her.

Rocío opened her mouth to add her reassurances but paused. She thought she'd heard Silvia shouting. Hala cocked her head.

Rocío stepped closer to the edge and looked down. Silvia pounded up the gangplank. Even from here Rocío could see she was red and frantic, sweat shining on her scalp through her butchered hair. Rocío felt a premonition of disaster. "Silvia," she called, willing the young advocate to be discreet.

"Pilar, are you here?" Silvia shouted, the opposite of discretion.

A moment of shocked silence and then the crew members erupted with a roar, converging on her.

"Oh, no." Rocío groaned.

Buenaventura slid down the banisters without touching the stairs, thumped to the deck and plunged into the shouting crowd, thrusting her crew members out of the way. With one hand she plucked the advocate from the crowd and with her other slapped the sternum of a man grabbing for Silvia. He staggered back, gasping. Hala almost slid down the steep stairs in her haste, and Rocío followed her.

Buenaventura pushed Silvia at Hala and stood like a wall between her and the crew. "Explain, Advocate," she snapped. The crew fell into a tense silence, willing to let her handle it, for now.

Silvia wheezed. "Is she here?"

"What?" Hala asked.

Rocío's heart thumped with dread.

"Pilar. I lost her."

CHAPTER 5

Rocío and Hala banged through the double doors into the admittance area of the University Hospital, expecting the barely controlled chaos of a response to another biological attack on the city. The Hospital had been the crisis center during the attack in November and should be able to ramp up operations quickly.

The waiting room was quiet. Tranquil even.

At their abrupt entrance, the nurse stationed near the doors jumped, knocking papers onto the floor.

A few people stopped their quiet conversations and looked up curiously. There was one other nurse at the far desk, and none of the activity presaging preparations for an influx of a large number of gravely ill people. A barely audible hum of voices and machines on the other side of the doors leading into the main treatment area indicated a normal amount of activity.

Disturbed, Rocío flashed her ID booklet at the nearest nurse, a young man with glossy brown hair. "We're from Miraflores CJC. You have someone in quarantine. Where is he? The patient's name is Costas from *The Resolute*. He's river folk."

"Quarantine?" he asked, his forehead crimping under the little white cap with a black band. "I just came on shift." He gathered the papers from the floor and led them across the room to the older nurse. "Do you know anything about a patient in quarantine?"

"We're detectives from Miraflores CJC," Hala repeated, showing her ID booklet.

The older nurse closed her folder and put it on the desk. Her graying hair and white cap, this one with a silver pip on the band denoting seniority, were more reassuring than the first nurse's smooth youth. "You'll want to talk to Doctor Andrade. Don't worry, it's not as dire as all that."

"Don't worry?" Rocío asked.

MMFs in the city with the main suspect now missing and the Hospital failing to react, and the nurse wanted her to not worry? Now was definitely the time to worry.

Hala closed her hand over Rocío's clenched fist and murmured, "You might want to watch your emotional reaction to the situation, Rocío. Let's just see what she says."

"Right." Rocío forced her hands to relax and stopped almost treading on the older nurse's heels as they walked down the corridor.

On the other side of the big double doors, the hum of activity increased, but to Rocío's ear, tuned in crisis, it was an everyday hum, not a crisis hum.

"Doctor Andrade, you said?" Hala asked.

The name gave Rocío another handle on her emotions. Doctor Andrade had treated her when she was infected with quick-onset malaria last November. He had saved their lives — and the lives of many others — with his innovative methods. If anyone had the situation under control, it was Doctor Andrade.

The nurse stopped at small ward, only ten beds, and caught Doctor Andrade's attention. In spite of his large size and gray hair he trotted lightly across the room to them. Costas was not in any of the beds.

"Rocío, Hala, that is you." He grasped their hands in turn, raising them for a quick look at the scars on their backs. "These look good. How are you? No lingering problems?" He accepted their quick demurrals and moved on. "Not here for a check up, are you?" His dark eyes glinted behind his spectacles as he assessed them.

"No, we're here about one of your patients." Hala lowered her voice. "Costas of *The Resolute*."

46

"And his sister, Pilar. A woman with two children," Rocío added. "Have you seen her? The advocate from Sanblas said she disappeared."

"Costas, of course, I should have guessed you'd be involved with that. I never actually saw the sister or the children. The nurses were changing shift and that means paperwork for me. You haven't found the woman? Your young advocate was very distressed."

That was putting it mildly. Silvia had almost been in hysterics, even more so when they told her they'd found an MMF. She immediately grasped the implications that Pilar's disappearance made her look guilty and made her the number one suspect. In the best case, Silvia had let Pilar escape justice; in the worst case, Pilar might continue her attacks.

They had lost valuable time sending the two chaskis for backup to keep the rest of the crew on the boat. They'd also had to hold the crew in check after a few of Silvia's inopportune comments about family loyalty. The one small mercy was that the crowd on the docks was not there to whip up the mess into even frothier heights of belligerence and suspicion. Khadija had had added responsibilities: delivering the MMF—discreetly wrapped in brown paper inside an old carpet bag—the captain's log and messages to their own CJC asking for backup at the Hospital and to start looking into Silvia's background.

There was something wrong there beyond new advocate nerves. Silvia had looked terrified; more terrified than losing a suspect warranted. They had tasked her with sending messages to all the CJCs throughout the city to be on the lookout for Pilar, again backed up by Khadija at their own CJC, in case Silvia's behavior wasn't just odd but criminal. Though whether conspiring with Pilar or if she had actually hurt Pilar in some way was the question. One of the questions. Silvia had also dodged Rocío's request that she start questioning locals and was instead confirming the movements of Pilar's boat, *The Resolute*, at the harbormaster's office.

A patient vomited. Hala put her hand over her nose as the smell reached them. Doctor Andrade said, "Let me show you something." He led them into the hall, maneuvering around orderlies pushing a gurney with a patient whose breath wheezed in his chest.

He turned into a long wardroom with a row of beds against one wall under windows open to admit light and air, aided by the fans whirling industriously from the corners and mounted on the walls. One creaked with every rotation and a worker stretched from the top of a ladder to reach it. Rocío hoped he'd shut it off before trying to fix it. About half the beds were occupied. In spite of the fresh air, it still smelled of antiseptic and ill-health. A few patients lay unmoving, eyes closed and pain worn into their faces, but most were sitting up, playing cards or talking with visitors.

Costas was off to the right, in the second bed on the left. He appeared to be unconscious. The two brothers from the boat were still with him. Victor, the younger one, sat next to Costas, leaning forward, his elbows on his knees and his head hanging. Sujay, the one with the beard that overwhelmed his face, leaned against the wall next to the window, his arms crossed over his chest, watching everything. At the sight of Rocío and Hala, he lurched forward, his fists clenching, a guttural growl caught in his throat. His brother shot to his feet, his chin jutting out with hostility.

Unsure whether this sudden aggression was directed at the doctor or herself, Rocío blocked Doctor Andrade with her arm to keep him from getting closer. Hala bracketed him on the other side.

"What's the matter?" Rocío asked, the question lost in the noise of several more people entering the room. Zhou and Perez, the advocates from the CJC Rocío had sent for, and the nurse with the shiny hair.

The two river folk surged towards Zhou and Perez. The advocates shouldered aside the young male nurse. He muffled an exclamation and stepped back, hugging a stuffed animal to his chest.

Advocate Zhou seized Sujay, the burly muscles in his arm standing out as he held Sujay in place. "Let's keep this calm."

Advocate Perez planted himself in front of Victor and stared him down from his superior height.

Victor tried to to push forward. "You—"

Perez planted his palm against Victor's shoulder, halting him.

48

"I was just returning this." The nurse brandished the stuffed animal, a gray bunny with floppy ears. "One of the children must have dropped it."

Rocío didn't recognize the toy, but the men from the boat clearly did and the tension ratcheted up.

"Where did you get that?" Sujay demanded. "That's Pilar's son's. Where is he?"

"I found it on the floor." The nurse gestured to the corridor. "Out there."

Victor broke desperately for the door. Perez was on him before he took more than five steps. In a blur of motion too quick to follow, Perez dropped Victor to the floor with one arm twisted behind his back. Victor grunted and jerked.

Perez bit out, "Don't try it."

Breathing heavily, the crew member collapsed in surrender. "I'm going to cuff you," Perez said. He clasped the restraints efficiently and impersonally and then lifted the crew member into a sitting position.

Rocío felt unexpectedly guilty. She'd sent these men to the hospital for care, and now she was taking them into custody. She hardened her heart against it. *If they're bringing a plague to my city they don't deserve leniency.* And everyone on their boat was in de facto custody, so she didn't know why she was upset now.

"What was that?" Rocío demanded of Victor.

"Nothing." He stared at his knees. "I thought you were going to arrest us."

"And now you're arrested," Rocío said more harshly than she'd intended.

Hala stepped into the center of the little tableau, forcing everyone who could to step back. Victor pulled his legs in. Hala stabbed a finger at Costas. "Doctor Andrade, why isn't there mosquito netting around him? You're not taking the proper measures and you're risking your other patients and the general population."

Rocío made eye contact with Zhou and Perez, checking in. They both gave her short nods. Zhou kept his hand on Sujay, who had his head turned away. The tendons stood out in his neck.

Satisfied that the Miraflores advocates would stay watchful and prevent any further unwise moves by the brothers, Rocío turned her attention to Costas. She was surprised to see his hands and arms weren't bandaged. He had been cleaned, the dirt and sweat removed from his skin, his hair brushed back from his face, and dressed in a hospital gown. As Hala had said, there was no netting or other measure to protect against the spread of the disease. While they didn't know if quick-onset malaria was transmitted by normal mosquitos biting an infected person, it wasn't a chance any doctor should be taking.

"Detective Haddad," Doctor Andrade said, taking a quick step forward and putting a protective hand on the iron frame of Costas's bed, "you should know me better than that. This man doesn't have quick onset malaria. He doesn't have malaria at all."

"What do you mean?" Rocío frowned doubtfully at the bites on the patient's arms.

"On what do you base your reasoning, Doctor?" Hala asked.

"This is what I wanted to show you," Doctor Andrade said. "Costas?" When there was no response he nodded to Sujay and said, "I'm going to touch him, just to show them what I showed you." He lifted one of Costas's arms, turning it to display the bite marks. Most were scabbed but one was raw and leaking blood.

"Gloves?" Hala asked.

Dr. Andrade indicated a wooden chest of drawers equidistant between Costas's bed and the next one.

Hala donned gloves, retrieved her magnifying glass and bent to peer through it. She straightened immediately in shock. "That's not a bite!"

Victor shuffled around and glared. Sujay said, "We didn't do that." His hands trembled.

"What?" Rocío asked. She grabbed the magnifying glass and looked through it but learned nothing for her effort. "What do you mean?"

"It's clearly a cut, very small and made to look like a bite, but the edges are wrong," Hala said.

Rocío took another look a the raw red mark and gave up. "I'll take your word for it."

"It was probably made by a small knife. Even a scalpel," Dr. Andrade said. "And there's more. The patient doesn't have malaria, either regular or quick onset. Despite efforts to make it look like he does."

"What?" Rocío asked, falling back a step. She had braced herself for a diagnosis of MMF-induced malaria and couldn't quite believe what she was hearing. She found herself meeting Sujay's eyes and the distress and fear she saw there helped her overcome her own confused emotions. She was the authority; she had the experience to do something about this, not just react. It was her job to do stop anyone depraved enough to threaten—or appear to threaten—the city in this way.

"Believe me, I saw enough cases to know. He doesn't have a fever."

"But—he was hot, sweaty, wouldn't wake up."

"We're also hot and sweaty," Dr. Andrade pointed out dryly.

"Detectives, what do we do about them?" Zhou asked, pointing to the two river folk.

Hala glanced around the ward. Although it was not crowded, it was full, and the interaction was the most interesting thing happening there. "Proceed as before. We still have an emergency to deal with."

"We didn't cause this emergency," Victor said, tension coiling through his body. "Ask..." he glanced from the advocates, to the patients, the nurse, who had bent to smooth the sheet back over Costas's chest, to the doctor. "Ask the doctor."

"Unfortunately I can't say who did this to him, or what exactly *this* is. Just what it is *not* at this point," Doctor Andrade said apologetically.

"Zhou, take them to the CJC." Rocío turned Victor. "Tell him everything you know. We'll get to the bottom of this."

There was no trust or belief in his eyes, just despair and betrayal.

Guilt flared again, even more muddled than before. On the one hand, if someone was attempting to incite panic in the city, as an advocate she had to do everything in her power to protect its citizens. On the other, she didn't go around putting innocent people into custody. She let the guilt settle, reminding herself to use it as a guidepost to her actions in what was no doubt going to be a very confusing situation.

"We serve everyone, Benerex and river folk." Rocío tried to impress her sincerity on him, without much hope for success.

"Then serve Costas," Sujay said. "Protect him."

"Do you know who incapacitated him?" Hala asked.

Sujay shook his head, his lips pressed together so hard they completely disappeared into his beard.

Perez lifted Victor from the floor and escorted him out the door. Victor craned his head to keep Costas in his sight for as long as possible.

Doctor Andrade sighed. "I wish you hadn't done that here. Nurse, can you check on the other patients? Make sure they're not too distressed."

"Yes, Doctor Andrade." He left the toy on the table next to Costas and moved to the next patient.

"Doctor, how sure are you?" Hala asked. "The blood test for malaria takes some time, correct?"

"You're right, I need the test results, but I looked at several of the 'bites' as the nurses cleaned him and they're all like that."

Rocío shifted restlessly with the need to act, realized this was the thing she needed to do and focused on Doctor Andrade again. Hala cupped her chin with one hand, hiding her mouth and most of her expression, but her eyes crinkled with worry.

Doctor Andrade looked around to see if anyone was in hearing distance. He leaned forward and spoke in a low voice. "Someone went to a great deal of trouble to make it look like MMF-induced malaria."

"You have no idea," Rocío muttered, thinking of the MMF body on its way to the forensics team. She lowered her voice even further. "We found an MMF."

He rocked back on his heels. "You did?"

"You can see why we're concerned," Hala said.

He adjusted his spectacles. "No. I stand by my diagnosis. My earlier statement stands."

"What is wrong with him?" Hala asked.

"My suspicion is poison. We're running tests: urine, hair, stomach contents and dosing him with activated charcoal in the hopes that it will bind with whatever poison he has in his system."

They digested that in silence for a moment. This changed everything. Someone—Pilar?—was attempting to make it look like the MMFs were back in La Bene. Why? What did they hope to gain? Was Costas the victim or the culprit? What about Pilar? Why had she run and where? Or were the river folk a convenient scapegoat because of the general prejudice against them?

"Will he regain consciousness?" Hala asked.

"And tell us who did this?" Doctor Andrade frowned down at Costas. "At this point I can't tell you. It depends on whether we can identify the poison—if it is one—and counteract it."

"How likely is it that another doctor would have come to the same conclusion as you?" Hala asked.

He scratched the back of his neck. "Well...we started an emergency medicine unit after the MMFs, so it's very likely that I or another doctor familiar with the symptoms would be called to consult. Very likely."

"What if you weren't called to consult?" Hala asked.

"And how many people know you started this emergency medicine unit?" Rocío asked. "I didn't."

"It depends," he admitted. "A doctor who hadn't seen the real bite marks might not have looked closer. And we haven't publicized the unit yet. The hospital is still testing. It's a radical new theory, though if you ask me, it's working."

Rocío couldn't see how fake malaria and a real MMF body fit together. Or where someone had gotten an MMF in the first place. She had been sick and directly involved in capturing the rogue doctor; she had not been involved in the clean up at all. She would have to check the files to see what had happened while she was in the Hospital recovering.

"Send us a message immediately if he regains consciousness," Hala said. "Meanwhile, would you assign someone to smell him, every four hours or so?"

That was not the weirdest thing Hala had ever said, but Rocío had no idea what it meant.

Doctor Andrade seemed to; his mouth opened slightly in surprise. "You think...oh yes." His mouth firmed. "I should have thought of that."

"I'm sure you would have," Hala said.

He looked around and focused on the nurse. "You, you're new. What's your name?" He stepped away.

"What am I missing?" Rocío asked Hala quietly.

"There are certain poisons that give off particular odors as they metabolize in the body. Doctor Andrade may be able to identify the poison, which would allow him to treat the patient appropriately."

"Tell the head nurse I want you here every four hours to smell this patient," Doctor Andrade finished his directions to the nurse, who murmured agreement and moved to the next patient. Most had returned to their games or conversations.

Doctor Andrade turned back to Rocío and Hala, his big hands clenched on the lapels of his coat. "I keep thinking I've seen everything in this job and then something new shocks me. There's no bottom to the depths of depravity humans will sink to. Using poison to try to panic the city... you have to find them and stop them."

CHAPTER 6

Rocío and Hala spent the next few hours in the Sanblas district, quelling rumors and looking for someone, anyone, who had seen— or attacked—Costas between when he left *The Resolute* and when he had returned on Thursday night, while other advocates searched for Pilar and found and returned the remaining crew members to the boat.

The official explanation, trotted out at every warehouse, tavern and food stall was that the river folk were suspected of smuggling and the rumors of MMFs were just that, just like the rumor the week before and the week before that. People were fatigued by reoccurring waves of plague panic, and were happy to dismiss their fears and return to normal life. The explanation did nothing for the river folk's reputation or the prejudice against them, but Rocío didn't see any other viable option. If she'd learned anything as an advocate, and especially during the plague, it was that sometimes compromises had to be made to protect the greater number of people, and individuals sometimes suffered. The decision was harder this time, with a marginalized group suffering the consequences, but they'd checked with the deputy chief of Miraflores CJC and it was her call. Rocío didn't disagree; she just didn't like it.

Chaskis ran back and forth with messages. Khadija was sent home, according to the laws governing child labor, and others replaced her. Late in the day, a Miraflores chaski ran up with the news that several of the crew members had tried to fight their way off the boat, begged the advocates keeping them there to get Costas out of the Hospital, swearing that he'd die there and that they had a right to refuse treatment. That decision wasn't Rocío's to make either, and she was glad of it.

Everyone had an opinion on the river folk; no one had information. At least none the residents of Sanblas—sailors, fishers, dockworkers, vendors—would give two detectives from Miraflores. Rocío recognized the sidelong looks and the closed off body postures, arms crossed, bottles or tables or counters a barrier between advocates and citizens, the belligerent stares. They spent some time looking for Silvia's aunt from the dock with the hopes she would smooth their way, but that also proved fruitless.

"This is why I wanted Silvia to do this," Rocío said, huffing her breath out in frustration as they left another tavern. She pushed sweaty locks of hair back into their pins, though they were going to fall out if she didn't completely redo her hair, and took a deep breath, smelling the river, dead fish, horse manure and the reek of human activity, but at least it was thinned by lots of air, unlike the atmosphere of the tavern, thick with tobacco smoke and old beer. Her clothes must reek but at least she could no longer smell herself. "Give me musicians and actors any day." Miraflores's area included the entertainment district as well as the neighborhoods surrounding the seat of government in La Bene. "They're easier to deal with. At least they talk."

"Even if it's mostly nonsense?"

"I feel like I'm the stage crew in an endless production of *Waiting on Waiting*."

"And you never had a leading role in that play," Hala said caustically. The day was wearing on her too.

"Hey." Rocío blocked Hala's forward motion. She felt like a windup toy that had fallen off the edge of a table but was still kicking its little feet. Two women pushed past, grumbling about Rocío blocking the sidewalk, and she pulled Hala out of the way, into the doorway of a shop that was already closed for the day. "This isn't getting us anywhere, and there are Sanblas advocates doing it better than we can."

Hala looked up at the sunset-streaked sky—lemon yellow and fiery pink and a dark red at the horizon— and then at her pocket watch. "It's late." Stating the obvious was a measure of how surprised she was and only reinforced how immersed Hala had been in their task. She shook out her shoulders. "I believe I haven't been thinking very clearly. Just the threat of," she cleared her throat and looked around. Even though none of the passing pedestrians appeared to be listening she avoided the words, "you know, has affected my thinking process."

Rocío's stomach growled. "And lack of food must be addling mine."

Hala cracked a smile.

They both looked around to orient themselves, though it had nothing to do with physical location and everything to do with read-justing internal paradigms. The cobblestone street teemed with horse-drawn carriages, sailors with canvas duffles on their shoulders, shoppers with bright green cilantro and epazote bristling out of their bags, and some kind of motorized cart that made a putt-putt-putt sound.

"Isn't there a restaurant with fish chowder that you like near the harbormaster's office?"

"You think Silvia is still at the harbormaster's, after all this time?"

Hala might agree they needed a break, but that didn't mean it couldn't be a strategic one that accomplished more than one thing at a time.

"Unless another chaski comes upon us who can supply an answer, I think the question is worth pursuing."

Just then a chaski with the Sanblas badge pinned to the shoulder of her huiple ran up. Hala arched an eyebrow at Rocío.

"Detectives Díaz and Haddad?" the boy puffed out.

"Yes," Hala said.

"Message for you."

The paper was damp from his sweat and unsealed. Hala held it so Rocío could read it at the same time.

They exchanged a glance. Hala's face was studiously blank, but her posture always shortened on the left side, her hip hitching up, when she was worried.

"Now we really need to find Silvia," Rocío said neutrally for the chaski's benefit. There was no way he hadn't read this unsealed note.

"Do you know where she is?" Hala asked him.

He shook his head, his eyes and mouth wide. They needed to find Silvia before the gossip did.

Hala tapped her finger against her lips. Rocío guessed she was weighing whether to question the boy about whether Silvia was liked at Sanblas CJC and whether this was real information, malice directed at her or something else entirely. Rocío shook her head slightly. The boy was too young, and she didn't judge it worth the extra gossip.

"We're on our way," Hala told him. "No other message."

"Don't forget to drink water," Rocío shouted after him.

They walked to the end of the block and turned left. "I think we've been letting our emotions dictate our behavior," Rocío finally said, going back to the previous conversation.

"I believe you're correct. It's something we should be on guard against."

"I keep hoping the world will go back to normal." Rocío trailed her hand over the wall of the warehouse that dominated this stretch of the street, relishing the alternating textures: rough stone, smoother mortar. "I didn't use to worry so much. And I didn't jump to judgement so quickly. About immigrants or foreigners. I'm suspicious of them in a way I wasn't before. I don't like it and I know it's wrong, but it keeps happening."

"At least you keep examining your emotions and reactions. Many people don't. And unfortunately we all carry abnormal within us now, in the form of memory and scars." Hala rubbed the ones on her hands, her lips pinching in at the corners. "And in our reactions."

Rocío checked the street before stepping off the curb into an opening in the foot and vehicle traffic. She waited until they reached the other side before responding. "You're saying there will always be a before and an after."

"Yes. But we have lived through befores and afters. Whether personal or society-wide." Hala sounded detached, the way she did covering up strong emotion.

"I know. I'm just getting tired. Bone tired you know?"

"I know." Hala hooked her arm through Rocío's. Sweat fused the skin on their bare arms immediately, but Rocío didn't pull away from Hala's offered comfort. Neither did Hala.

A few minutes later, Rocío said with forced cheer, "The Chowder House. And look, there's no line. Come on." She tugged Hala forward in a quick walk.

"You don't have to do that for me," Hala said. "Pretend."

"Oh, it's not for you," Rocío lied with a smile. "It's all for me."

Hala narrowed her eyes at Rocío, not accepting it for a minute, but let it pass.

The Chowder House served one kind of chowder and the only options were crackers or no crackers. Rocío opted for with and Hala without. They sat on the low wall facing the river, though it was barely visible here through the crowd of ships, like the audience for the mid-season opera, when some of the best performances were discounted and people from every strata of society could afford to go, and did. At the opera the audience was clad in silk or cheap cotton, with real gems in their hair or paste or enamel; some of the ships here were the silk equivalent, tall, gleaming with a forest of masts and deceptively tangled-looking rigging for the ocean voyages to the Poly Poly Islands, Iberon or far Jeen, while others were cheap cotton, peeling paint and mismatched sails, low to the water, but adept at slipping through crowds, and traveling a limited circuit of tens of kilometers, not tens of thousands.

Rocío crumbled her crackers into the chowder and inhaled the scents of tomato, garlic and pepper. Here, beside the river where the brown of its upriver silt mixed in streamers with the blue of the ocean, the small tender clams tasted like the scenery itself. Briny umami balanced by the earthy taste of the potatoes.

"Are you rhapsodizing over your food again?" Hala asked. She sounded better. When Rocío checked, Hala's cheap pottery bowl was already empty.

"You should be. Do you know how lucky we are to get this kind of food?"

"Hmm."

"Okay, do you know how lucky you are I wasn't rhapsodizing out loud?" Rocío scraped up the last of her soup and contemplated licking it.

"Don't embarrass me," Hala warned.

That decided it. Rocío licked as much of the bowl as she could and then made a show of licking her lips. "Mm mm good."

Hala shuddered in disgust, but she also laughed. "Come on."

They returned the rough clay bowls and spoons. Rocío's steps didn't drag as much as before and her thinking felt clearer. "So, do you think Silvia is involved?"

"I dislike coincidences, but when all's said and done, La Bene only has a population of 350,000. The population of Sanblas is just under 5,000 permanent residents, swelling to 15,000 when you count the transient sailors and the native Benerex who commute from other parts of the city to work here."

"You're saying we need to talk to Silvia and her father," Rocío said, interpreting Hala speak.

"Yes, that's what I just said."

The harbormaster's office was on one end of the customs and immigration building that occupied an entire block of Avenida Zeisel. The front was made up of open counters where mariners could line up. You only got into the offices behind the counter if a clerk let you. Or forced you. The harbormaster's offices at the rear had their own entrance, which was guarded by a massive desk and a little clerk just inside.

"We're closed," she said without looking up. "Unless it's an emergency."

"We're Detectives Díaz and Haddad from Miraflores CJC," Hala said. "Is Advocate Silvia Dante Ruíz still here?"

The clerk squinted at Hala, and then lowered her spectacles from where they rested on the top of her head and took another look. "Are you here to take her away?"

"Yes."

"Then come right this way." She popped up, leaned on the heavy wooden door to open it and led them to a small room. It was oppressively lined with shelves on all four walls that were stuffed with black and brown ledgers. The lack of windows made it even more claustrophobic. Silvia sat at another heavy desk that barely fit in the space. Ledgers were spread out in front of her and stacked at the edges like a barricade.

"Detectives!" She had dust smudged on one cheek and more shadows under her eyes than could be explained by the placement of the light fixtures. "Um, sorry, but could you give us a minute?" she asked the clerk.

"As long as it's the last minute," the clerk said. "I need to close this room."

As soon as the door thudded shut behind the clerk, Silvia surged to her feet and leaned across the table. "Detectives, it's MMFs for sure!"

Startled, Rocío barked her knee on the table and stopped with her mouth open, trying to adapt her thinking. Hala managed it first.

"Why do you say so?"

Rocío probably would have led with "It is not."

Hala's response sounded much more dignified and likely to elicit answers.

Silvia motioned them closer. She checked the covers of two ledgers and then pulled a third from underneath them. "Look at this." She drummed her finger on one of the entries. The ledger was a record of who had left La Bene by boat and the date they had done so. The line Silvia pointed to read Doctor Hector Collins, native of

Enkladt, 4 October 446, *The Resolute*, Captain Costas, destination Kooja Ya.

Hector Collins, the man responsible for creating the malarial mosquito fairies in Enkladt, unleashing them on La Bene, killing at least fifty people, and terrorizing the city, had been on Pilar's boat three years ago.

CHAPTER 7

BACK ON THE STREET, Silvia seemed subdued. She hadn't taken the news well that her big discovery only confused the issue more, and Rocío hadn't offered any of the encouragement she usually gave new advocates because she wasn't sure if Silvia was a suspect or a colleague.

As they threaded through a pack of loudly arguing factory workers on bicycles, Rocío watched the young advocate with narrowed eyes. Silvia hadn't spoken since they left the harbormaster's office. And then there was the way she moved, angling so no one bumped her left arm and flinching away from unexpected movements almost before they happened.

Rocío compared it with her memory of the morning. The arm was new. But so much had been happening on the boat, she wasn't sure if it had happened while Silvia was at the Hospital or after. The flinching wasn't new, but it was more pronounced now. It could be hypervigilance stemming from the renewed threat of MMFs. Half the Miraflores advocates had been as jumpy as a cat in traffic after the November attack, Rocío included. But it also reminded Rocío uneasily of the way victims of abuse acted.

The people most likely to abuse others were family members or romantic partners. If Silvia's father was abusing her, just bringing the two together could be ugly, and Rocío might be risking Silvia's safety.

On the other hand, if Silvia was a suspect they couldn't just leave her. And if she was being hurt they couldn't just leave her either, no matter what she had done or not done.

So they still had to follow the lead about Silvia's father.

Decision made, Rocío tapped Hala on the shoulder in their signal for possible danger. Hala dipped her chin, her glance going from Rocío to Silvia and back. Rocío touched her own left arm, and the lines around Hala's mouth deepened. She circled her finger on her own chest, in the place where even in summer many Benerex wore a tupu, the large, ornate pin used to hold closed a shawl or serape in winter. Sure enough, when Rocío looked, there were holes in Silvia's huiple where Hala had indicated. Lovers sometimes exchanged the pins, and a missing one might also point to a relationship recently ended on bad terms.

Silvia turned to Hala, who wiped the considering frown from her face. "Where are we going?"

"The Fishers' Club. There's someone there we need to talk to. We thought you'd be able to help since you know the people in this district."

Silvia hunched her shoulders and didn't answer.

Hala led them up Avenida Zeisel, warehouses giving way to restaurants and taverns on their right, and the deep-water ships on their left yielding to shorter, more contingent docks thickly crowded with the smaller local fishing boats. A few deserted docks trailed lines into the water, left by the fishers who sailed at night.

In the midst of all this clutter, one pier stretched out almost two hundred meters in relatively solitary splendor, crowned with a stucco and timber mini chateaux, topped with a red tile roof and a fishing rod flying a red flag, all silhouetted against the setting sun. The Fishers' Club, open to members only. Rocío had never had occasion to enter, either in her official capacity or as a guest of a member.

"I've always wondered..." Rocío bent sideways, trying to get a glimpse of sewage pipes beneath the pier. "What do they do with the waste?"

Twilight was creeping up the river, making it too dark to see underneath the structure, but old-fashioned lanterns illuminated a floating dock on the downriver side where small boats could tie up and restaurant-goers could ascend to the club via a ladder.

"It's ingenious really," Hala began. Her lecture on sewage, gravity and plumbing took them all the way to the door of the Fisher's Club, where Hala finally took pity on Silvia's dubious expression and stopped.

Inside, the host recognized Silvia, and Rocío looked around while they talked. The wooden and brass furnishings shone with polish and care, though they were not fancy. Strategically placed warm electric lights illuminated photographs and paintings of fishers, the river and the sea, a gleaming black baby grand piano and an enormous aquarium. The fisher paraphernalia Rocío half expected—nets, floats and buoys—were absent. About twenty people sat at sturdy round tables generating a low hum of conversation. Rocío sniffed the aromas of citrus, frying garlic and fish appreciatively. It was a far cry from the dank taverns they'd spent the afternoon in.

Silvia turned to Hala. "Who do you want to talk to?"

"Your father Alejandro."

"My papi?" Silvia squeaked. "Is he in trouble?"

"Silvia, you're an advocate, you know that we don't only talk to people because they're in trouble," Hala said.

Silvia bit her lip, not looking convinced, but she squared her shoulders and led them to a table facing the dark expanse of water.

The river was so wide here that the far bank wouldn't be visible even during the day. On this side of the restaurant, the lights of the city were no more than brief reflections on the water.

The two men sitting there looked up and smiled broadly at Silvia.

"These are my fathers," Silvia said.

"Sil," a balding man said, standing. He had the beefy arms and shoulders of a dockworker and when he pulled Silvia into a hug she almost disappeared into his embrace.

"Papi, I'm working," Silvia said, the words muffled against his chest.

"Sorry, mija, I forget." He released her, and her other father put a hand on her hip, smiling fondly up at her. He was just as muscled, but had more hair than the other man, coiled and pinned with warm amber pins in the style used by all genders in La Bene. The shape of his nose and something about the eyes bespoke their biological relationship, though the familial relationship with both was obvious. Neither man made Silvia flinch, and she had concealed the pain to her arm that hug must have caused. Both men wore matching inexpensive copper tupus, the long thick pin stuck through their huiples, the head in the shape of simple leaf.

The hugger introduced himself as Alejandro Dante Murillo, the one who had been seen with Costas.

"And I'm Enzo Ruíz García," the other said, offering his hand.

It was still possible, of course, that one of Silvia's fathers was hurting her, but Rocío was very good at reading body language and she hadn't seen fear or hesitation in Silvia, or dominance and control in the fathers.

She relaxed a little and let Hala do the talking, so she could observe. Helping someone deal with an abusive parent was a lot more complicated than if the abusive person was a lover, though neither was easy. It seemed more and more likely they were looking at the latter, though how that intersected with Pilar's disappearance, Rocío couldn't guess yet.

She was finally getting used to the shock of Silvia's shorn hair, enough to really look at the young woman. Silvia's skinniness was also more apparent next to her fathers' robust health. Again, it could be that she was still a teenager or another sign of abuse.

"So what are you doing here, then, talking to us, if you're working?" Enzo asked.

Silvia slanted a look at Rocío and Hala. "They need to ask you some questions, Papi."

"Me?" Alejandro asked, fiddling with his tupu. Suddenly alert, Enzo leaned back from his spouse. Silvia moved so she could see both her fathers' faces.

"We're searching for information about a river folk captain," Rocío said easily. "We were told you might be able to help us."

Alejandro's gaze slid away from Rocío, shifting between Silvia and Enzo. "I don't know how I can help, I don't know any river folk, captains or not."

"Silvia, would you ask the host if Costas was here on Thursday?" Rocío interjected.

"Papi, did you do something?"

"It's not like that, Sil."

Silvia flounced away and cornered the host.

"Would you give us a moment, Señorx?" Hala asked Enzo.

Rocío slid her hand into the crook of Alejandro's arm and tugged gently, suspecting he wanted to respond to her urging and get away from his spouse's now openly suspicious expression.

"Enzo, I..."

"It will only take a moment," Hala said.

Rocío drew Alejandro to the end of the bar where busboys returned empty glasses. She indicated the bartender should stay at the other end and that Hala should stand farther away from Alejandro so he wouldn't feel boxed in. "Now, what didn't you want to say in front of your family?"

"Nothing." Avoiding Rocío's gaze, he pulled his arm free.

She let him and leaned casually on the bar, stacking the coasters she found there. "We just need some information."

"Unless you have committed a crime as egregious as murder, we're not interested in arresting you, if that's your concern," Hala said softly.

"Murder!" He stiffened and met Rocío's eyes for the first time since she had said they had questions. There were lines of strain around his eyes. Rocío kept her expression nonjudgemental and expectant.

After a moment he rubbed his hand over his balding head. "Nothing like that. I saw your river folk captain on Thursday. I didn't want Enzo knowing who I was here with." He sagged against the bar and mumbled, "I was with Dirty Eddy, the bookie? I owe him money."

Rocío turned to look at Silvia, the pieces rearranging themselves in a new possible configuration. "Has Dirty Eddy threatened your daughter, Señorx?" Rocío asked through tight lips.

"What? No! It's just cockfighting, not that much money. Enzo doesn't approve..." He seemed to really look at his daughter, who was biting her lip and tugging at her long sleeves. "She looks bad." He sounded surprised. "She said the hair was an accident with glue and a suspect, but she looks like she's been doing hard labor. Things haven't been right for... a while." He stared at Silvia with a pained expression.

When he didn't say anything else, Hala prompted, "The river folk captain. Costas."

"Right, yeah."

He turned so he wasn't staring directly at his daughter, but Rocío noticed his feet still pointed at her. The feet didn't lie; his attention was barely on the detectives. Rocío waited to see if that would help or hinder the flow of information. Some of her tiredness was lifting at the prospect of a real lead and someone who was actually answering their questions.

"Is that his name? I didn't see him come in or who he was with, but when I went to take—uh, use the facilities back here, he was passed out in the restroom. We couldn't wake him up, but he smelled like aguardiente. Mario—the bartender—said there was only one river folk boat at the docks so we took him there."

"We?"

"Me and David. He also likes cockfighting so if you could not mention this to my family..." His gaze drifted over to his spouse.

"What did Costas's arms look like?" Hala asked.

Alejandro jerked his attention back and raised his eyebrows in confusion. "His arms? They looked normal."

"Did he have any cuts or bruises on them?"

"Oh." He crossed his own arms, considering. "Not that I could see. He had on bracers, on his forearms, like a lot of river folk. His face was okay and his knuckles weren't bruised or scraped like he'd been in a fight, if that's what you mean."

Rocío let his misunderstanding pass without comment. "Was he completely unconscious?"

"Yeah. We had to carry him."

"What about when you got him to the boat?"

"We couldn't get him up the gangplank—too narrow—so we put

him on the dock and shouted at the boat until someone came up. Then we cleared out, didn't want to get blamed for his condition."

"What time was all this?"

"I'm not sure. After nine. Maybe even after ten."

So Costas was ambulatory up until nine or maybe ten on Thursday night. The big question was had he been poisoned on his boat or after he left it? Until Doctor Andrade told them what kind of poison had been used, they didn't even know what time frame they should be asking about. He could have been poisoned days or even months ago with the effects only surfacing now. But the cuts on his arms had been fresh. And where did the MMFs and their original creator come into this?

Hala caught Rocío's eye and inclined her head slightly, first at Silvia, who stood, arms crossed, watching them intently, and then at the back where the restrooms were. It wasn't their usual division of labor, as Rocío usually did the questioning and Hala looked for physical evidence, but Rocío agreed with her assessment: Silvia was going to charge over the minute they were done with her father and it was better that Rocío talk to her with more privacy than the open dining room provided.

Hala joined the bartender. At her request he handed Rocío a flashlight before Hala began asking him about Thursday. Rocío got Alejandro's address and information about David. "I'm afraid Silvia will learn about the gambling, as she's involved in this investigation. It might be better if you told her yourself," she said before sending him back to his family. Keeping an eye on Silvia, she made her way to the restrooms.

Silvia grabbed her father's hand and asked him something urgently. He shook his head. Rocío lost sight of them as she entered the narrow corridor at the back. The flashlight produced a weak beam of yellow light that barely illuminated the floorboards and wasn't going to help her find any evidence almost five days old. Feeding the battery a spark of magic to recharge it didn't help.

"I have got to start carrying my flashlight or make Hala do it." Every advocate was issued a flashlight, but Rocío hadn't bothered to add hers to the heavy belt around her hips in the heat of midday. *Shortsighted.*

Just as she was judging the best place to kneel—the floor wasn't any dirtier than you'd expect with kitchen and restroom traffic but her knees were bare—Silvia charged into the corridor. Too soon for Alejandro to have come clean. Sighing, Rocío turned off the flashlight and arranged her body in an open, listening posture: relaxed, none of her limbs drawn up tight, fully facing Silvia, including her feet.

"What did you say to my papi, detective? You can't treat him like that!"

Rocío made a split second decision to be direct. "Is Dirty Eddy threatening you to get Alejandro's money?"

"No...what?" Silvia gaped at her.

"Then who did that to your hair?" Rocío asked gently. "I doubt you did it to yourself."

Silvia flinched and lifted her hand to her hair. She forced it down without touching. "Why are you asking me that?"

"I think you're in trouble, Silvia, and I'm trying to help."

Expression shuttering, Silvia drew back. The problem was that hiding something that was done to you and hiding something you did just looked like hiding.

"Did Pilar bruise your arm before she disappeared?" Rocío asked, still gently.

Silvia didn't stop her reaction this time; she cradled her left arm in the right against her chest and hunched her shoulders, scrunching her head between them like that would hide her from Rocío. "No! She just disappeared. I was careless, okay, I let her go to the restroom by herself because I thought it was more important to stay by Costas, and I was wrong."

More than her words, Rocío believed her body language—it shouted out a pattern of repeated ongoing abuse, not a one time act of violence. Rocío used her most soothing, you-can-confide-in-me voice. Developed for her stage career, it transferred to public service very well. "Silvia, who hurt your arm and shaved your head? The same person who has your tupu?"

Tears sprang up in Silvia's eyes and she turned away to hide them. "I'm fine. It's fine."

Rocío waited to see if Silvia would answer on her own. She suspected Silvia had been coerced enough that any question might make her feel like she was backed into a corner again.

"It's over. I'm taking care of it," Silvia finally muttered, half belligerently, half ashamed.

"This is a complicated investigation. I need to know this isn't connected."

"It's not," Silvia muttered to her feet.

Rocío waited to see if she would say anything else and decided not to push any more for now. "I'm here if you want to talk about it." She signaled to Hala, who'd been hanging back for the last few minutes, not wanting to interrupt.

"Have you found anything?" Hala asked.

Silvia started and turned away to wipe her eyes.

"Not yet," Rocío said, knowing Hala would interpret that as commentary on Silvia as much as physical clues. She summed up her conversation with Alejandro, leaving all the personal details for later. Silvia's lips pinched together with exasperation. While Rocío talked, she nudged open the door to the empty restroom and swept the beam of the flashlight over the floor. Not that she expected discarded vials of poison or bloody knives after so long and regular cleaning— obvious from the faint smell of lemon and mothballs and the only mild scent of urine.

"Oh, píerdalo." Rocío swung back to Hala with a sudden thought. "Do we have to go talk to that unpleasant chemist again? What if Pilar really did steal a poison from her?"

"No, I looked through the list of stolen items the chemist submitted at her adjudication. None of them could account for Costas's condition, even if Pilar had stolen them. And she did pay for the quinine."

"Quinine?" Silvia pulled herself together and re-entered the conversation like someone nerving themselves for a plunge into frigid water. "Doesn't that mean she's innocent, if she was trying to treat malaria instead of poison?"

Hala looked around for anyone in hearing distance and knocked on the closed restroom door.

"Go piss in the river," a male voice shouted from inside.

"I haven't checked the end of the hallway," Rocío said, moving in that direction.

The others followed, Hala explaining quietly, "Unfortunately, the opposite. Quinine is also used as a preventative. She might have wanted it for herself."

Rocío found the exterior door more or less where she expected it. It opened onto a steep set of stairs with a gap between the last riser and the floating dock; the tide was out. The air smelled of brine and thick mud and pungent kerosene from the lanterns. One dingy and one larger fishing boat were tied to the dock. There was no attendant.

Rocío stepped out so Hala and Silvia could get a better view. The dock dipped beneath her feet with her weight. The absolute darkness of a night with no electrical lights seemed to fall towards Rocío, bringing her back to her childhood, before electric lights.

Hala joined her and turned in a circle to examine the surroundings from every angle. "The bartender said that as far as he can recall no one else was back here when Costas went to the facilities, but he was occupied with the costumers and was not certain. Dirty Eddy"—Hala said the words fastidiously—"was at the bar at the time. A few of the members were displeased Eddy had brought 'a foreigner and one of those river folk' to the club and there was a bit of an altercation. Dirty Eddy definitely brought Costas here. He signed the guestbook with Costas's name."

"A fight could cover the sounds of someone attacking Costas, if that's what happened. You think he was poisoned here?"

Hala shrugged. "It's a possibility. It would be easy to lie in wait for a man here, and though it's possible Costas walked across half of Sanblas already cut and poisoned, would he have taken off his bracers and then put them back on? Apparently they never have an attendant here. They believe in self regulation." The dock dipped with Hala's weight and Rocío gave her a hand up the first, higher, step.

"And the occasional fight," Silvia put in.

"As I said, self-regulation." Hala grinned at her and a tentative smile lifted the corners of Silvia's mouth.

"The bartender estimated that Costas was not in the main room for anywhere between five and thirty minutes. Five minutes is not much time for a paralytic or sedative, but thirty minutes is more than enough. He also gave me a list of names of everyone he remembers being here that night."

Hala's look at Rocío was a question, though Silvia probably couldn't tell. Rocío dipped her chin, and Hala handed Silvia a piece of paper. "Please take it to your chief and decide how to best organize finding and questioning them, including Dirty Eddy."

"Me?" Silvia looked from Hala to Rocío.

"You're a Sanblas advocate, aren't you?"

Hala might say her strongest skills were her memory, observation and ability to make connections between seemingly unrelated pieces of information, but she wasn't half bad at picking the right words to say in a completely matter of fact tone.

Silvia drew herself up. "Yes, I am."

One small step towards shoring up some badly eroded self-esteem, if Rocío wasn't mistaken. They had made progress today after all. Too bad more of it wasn't on the case.

CHAPTER 8

THE NIGHT CONCIERGE tipped back in his chair on the ground floor of Rocío's apartment building, a pulp novel spread open in front of him on the abbreviated counter, while he cracked roasted peanuts, thumbed them into his mouth and tossed the shells into a shellacked gourd.

"Hello, Jakob," Rocío said tiredly. Her face ached from all the talking, just like it had that season *Mathilde* had run a matinee and an evening performance three times a week. All she wanted was to flop into bed and sleep for ten hours, though that was wishful thinking.

At least the building seemed quiet, with most people asleep. It was full of people who couldn't or wouldn't—like Rocío—live in the big extended families that were the default for almost every ethnic group in the city. It made for an eclectic community, one Rocío usually enjoyed being a part of. On a night like this though, she was glad to avoid a prolonged discussion of the most popular tacata songs or who sold the best corn to make tortillas or whether it was acceptable to buy pre-made ones.

"Hi." Jakob examined her with short-sighted brown eyes. "Long day."

Rocío kept herself from checking her pocket watch. She didn't want to know what time it was besides late. "Yup." She moved past him towards the stairs.

"Wait," he called, his voice muffled.

She turned to find he had disappeared.

"I have packages for you," he said from under the desk. He banged his head on the way up. "Ow." He dropped a wide flat box, about as long as Rocío's arm, on the counter, followed by a shoe box, and rubbed his temple.

Both boxes were wrapped in brown paper with ink-stamped logos from Aurelian, a fancy clothing store. The sigh that escaped her seemed to take all her remaining energy with it and she leaned against the wall. The old Ka masons who had constructed the building centuries before the city became La Bene had used enormous stones, and on this hot summer night the slight chill they exuded was welcome.

There was only one—make that two people who would send her designer clothing. Her parents.

"You okay?" Jakob asked. "Your father wanted me to let him into your apartment but I remembered what you said. I told him there were new orders from the landlord, not to let anyone but residents in." He swept up stray peanut shells with swift, nervous motions and dropped them into the gourd. "That's what you wanted, right?"

"Yes. Thank you, Jakob. That's what I wanted." She patted his hand and the tension went out of him. *If only the tension would go out of me so easily.* Thank the seres celestiales Jakob hadn't let her father in. The last time he had dropped off a "gift" he also threw away her favorite shoes and rearranged her closet. It had taken her a whole day to find her earrings.

He grinned at her. "He didn't like it, but I kept my feet on my ground and didn't budge. Didn't try to explain either, like you suggested. He boomed a bit and puffed up. Is he really always like that?"

"He's really always like that." She pulled a handful of coins from her pocket and dropped them into his tip jar. "Did your daughter make that?" She gestured to the gourd. Its natural orange had been painted over in spots with bumbly purple flowers.

He nudged it with a finger, setting it rocking. "She sure did. Held the paintbrush all by herself."

"She's growing fast. I'll stop by when this case is over. Have a good night, Jakob." Rocío picked up the package with all the care she'd show a venomous snake and climbed the stairs.

Inside her apartment, she turned on the light in the kitchen alcove, pushed aside a stack of mail, a tea-stained script and her empty mug from the morning, and set the packages on the counter. Staring at them, she flexed her bare toes against the cool tiles of the floor, grounding herself. *If I'm smart, I'll go to bed and open them tomorrow. Or the day after.* Her parents' marriage contract signing party wasn't for almost two weeks. She didn't have to open them now. The boxes would nag at her attention, though eventually she'd fall asleep. But opening them wasn't a guarantee of quick slumber either. Rage wasn't conducive to sleep. Gifts from her parents had nothing to do with Rocío. Aurelian clothing tended to the pastel and frilly, appropriate for the daughter her parents wanted Rocío to be, not the daughter they had.

Without consciously making a choice, and knowing she would regret it, she reached for a knife and cut the string, getting some satisfaction from carelessly ripping the paper open across the designer logo.

The pale lavender dress looked so innocuous and not like a stab to the very center of the identity Rocío had created for herself, separate from her parents. But the color would suit Rocío's mother, with her lighter complexion and hair, and make Rocío look like she had a wasting disease. The frills would over-emphasize Rocío's muscled shoulders and the waist was punishingly small. Never mind that the style was more appropriate for a twenty year old and not a forty-three year old. Even the material was one Rocío didn't particularly like: a too-slick satin that brought back childhood memories of being clutched tightly to her mother's side in a display of affection. The shoes were a similar travesty.

Her fingers started to ache from gripping the edge of the counter so hard. She let go and shook them out.

She didn't know why she was surprised. They did this every time.

She shoved the packages away, sending a pile of mail fluttering to the floor, and bent, resting her forehead on the counter, hoping its coolness and the pressure would soothe the sudden ache behind her eyes.

The position suddenly felt too resigned and she stood up and paced away. That made her think of Isis, who would pace and break things and not even feel particularly bad about it later, as if the release of emotions was worth it. Rocío looked at her apartment, at the things she had picked out for herself: rose-tinted limewashed walls and layered amber-and-rose colored rugs, her collection of tea infusers in whimsical shapes and the paintings she'd bought in the plaza, bright slashes of people in motion, together. There was nothing here that she could stand to break.

Abruptly she stripped out of her clothes and dropped them to the floor. It took only a minute to find a bra and shorts to run in and she was out the door, down the stairs and out on the street. She knew she should warm up, but she stretched into a run immediately, letting the thud of her feet against the wooden sidewalks block out thought. The bodega on the corner was a bright spot of activity and talk, and she steered away. Sweat started to drip down her temples and her chest, into her cleavage, tickling.

Everything was a distraction, so she didn't have to think. Or feel. Bars, music, the sound of a fight, the sweet peppery smell of slow-roasted pork marinated in achiote and lime. The burn in her thighs, overcoming the burn in her throat of all the words she would choke on if she ever let herself think them.

CHAPTER 9

Rocío slung herself into her desk chair and winced at the pain in her lower back. She pressed her hands over her eyes. Oversleeping would seem to imply she had gotten enough sleep, but that wasn't true, and she hadn't had time to shower before work. She rubbed the crust from her eyes and slid her jaw back and forth to ease the tightness there. In spite of running herself into exhaustion, she hadn't slept well until dawn.

Hala appeared and dropped a brown paper bag from Benito's on the desk. She picked up Rocío's empty mug, frowned into it, blew out the dust and filled it from a thermos she had tucked under her other arm. The smell of Benito's coffee infinitesimally perked Rocío up.

Hala pulled plates out of her desk drawer and dumped out pastries: two bolas and two conchas, both de políticos, the off-color names of body parts deriding politicians and memorializing a turbulent period in the history of La Bene. Since Hala's idea of breakfast was labne and bread or other foods Rocío had once considered too savory for early in the morning, she knew this offering was for her.

The first rich sip of coffee was almost as good as stepping out on stage. The caffeine could not possibly act that fast, so it must be a learned response. Still, she'd take it.

"How did you know?" Rocío asked.

"I have my ways."

"Spying on me?"

"As if I needed to. You're more predictable than you think. If you're not here by five to nine, you'll be late."

"And I deluded myself that you were the one ruled by routines, and I was the erratic bohemian."

Hala snorted her opinion of that characterization.

Rocío cupped the mug for the emotional warmth; the morning was warm enough already. Balls, today, definitely balls. She crunched into one of the round pastries, anticipating the creamy filling that squeezed out and catching it on her fingers. Even anarchist-named pastries could be traditional, and cream filling was nothing but.

"Do you want to talk about it?" Hala asked. She examined Rocío with a look strangers took as almost clinical detachment, but Rocío knew the bone-deep caring hidden inside. "This is more than the incident yesterday, isn't it?"

"Is that what we're calling it?"

"Did something happen with your parents?"

Rocío chomped the last bite of the pastry and avoided Hala's eyes by taking a slow sip of coffee.

"Your father?" Hala's eyebrows went up at whatever she read on Rocío's face. She settled on the edge of Rocío's desk.

Hala was her best friend, her confidante for most things, but she was also relentless in her campaign against Rocío's self-centered parents. Still, they were *her* parents. So, did she talk, knowing anything she said would be used, whether in a powdered sugar sweet interrogation, or even a fusillade? And sometimes it took so much explanation. Apparently most parents didn't use gifts to control their children or as a weapon in a war Rocío had been fighting defensively since she was old enough to say "No."

But she didn't have the energy today to delay the inevitable. And secretly she enjoyed the outrage Hala could express more freely than Rocío ever could.

"It was about the party?"

Rocío contemplated putting her head on Hala's leg but pride won out over comfort. They were at work. Though it might make Hala feel so badly for Rocío it would distract her.

Khadija bounded into the room and made straight for their desks, temporarily saving Rocío from the emotional whiplash between loyalty to her birth family and the family of her heart. Khadija's dark hair was impeccably coiled and pinned in place with new hairpins that sparkled with glass gemstones, but she eyed Hala's cropped hair covertly before speaking.

"Yaco wants you to come down to lab three," she said.

"Oh, good," Rocío said too brightly. "We'll have to talk later."

Hala scowled at her. "I will find out."

"You always do." She patted Hala's arm, crammed a concha in her mouth and started for the courtyard.

Behind her she heard Hala offer one of the pastries to Khadija.

The heavy smell of roses nearly suffocated her as she cut through the interior courtyard that all the rooms opened onto. It was cooling in summer, and unfortunately also in winter. The bushes curled heavy with blooms over lattices and small frogs burped outsized frog burps in the central rain reservoir. This late in the summer the water level was fairly low. Hala and Khadija chatted behind her, something about the association their first-generation immigrant parents were members of.

Back inside, but now at the rear of the building, Rocío felt the layers of temperature in the air like a thousand layer cake as she descended the stairs until it was almost cool. Even in midsummer, the thick stone walls kept the heat out. The tech staff who worked down here were so lucky. Fans really didn't do much when the air they were moving was also hot. *Someone has got to invent something better.*

Outside of lab three the sign was flipped to "Other" with "autopsy," scrawled in. She paused. Not a procedure usually performed at the CJC; that was what a coroner's office was for.

"Oh, good, autopsy with breakfast," she said over her shoulder to Hala and Khadija.

The shelf next to the door held a jar of menthol and hair nets. She dabbed some of the ointment under her nose and pulled on a net. She'd managed to do her hair decently if nothing else, so that was easy enough. Bracing herself for the horrible smell and sights of a corpse that was cut open, she entered the room. "Hello, Yaco, I..."

For some reason she hadn't expected the little fairy body to be on the autopsy table, stretched out under a high intensity electric light. Several magnifying glasses clamped to the table obscured Rocío's view from this distance, like looking through a large aquarium from the corner. She glimpsed red and the glistening of viscera before she looked away.

Yaco looked up. "There you are. I—no, no, no. Khadija, get out and don't listen at the door."

She looked wounded. "Yaco, please—"

"No. And you're not to tell anyone what you saw in here. I mean it, Khadija, this is not a joke."

"I already know the secret!"

"I know. And that's the only reason you're not being confined to an interview room right now."

"Fine." Khadija tromped out in a huff and closed the door behind her.

"It's my fault," Hala said. "We were talking about the incompleteness theorem, which states that there are solutions to mathematical problems which are true but which can never be proved."

"Of course you were," Rocío said. Khadija was all of fourteen. Some of the tightness eased out of Rocío's back. There was nothing more normal in her life than Hala talking about something Rocío only vaguely understood. "Besides, what does it matter? She was with us yesterday. She already saw."

Yaco waved a hand in forgiveness. "Because I told her not to come in here. In a probably misguided attempt to control the rumors. The reappearance of a MMF has us all rattled and worried people gossip."

"All people gossip," Rocío said.

"You should know."

"Ouch."

He grinned at her, the familiarity of the exchange settling him, too. "Come here."

Hala took his invitation while Rocío boosted herself on one of the counters along the wall as far as she could get from the one that was standing in for an autopsy table. What was the word for animals? Hala would know. Necropsy? That sounded wrong too. Dissection?

"Yaco, why are you doing this? Where's the coroner?" Rocío asked.

"I asked him to." Hala grimaced. "The fewer people who know about this, the less likely that rumors will spread through the city."

"I think that ship has sailed."

Yaco ignored her. "I did a rotation with the coroner's office, and it's not human anyway." The non-humanness and the rotation with the coroner didn't keep him from looking pale or his Adam's apple from bobbing convulsively as he bent over the body. His usual job involved inanimate evidence, chemistry, magic analysis and innumerable iterations of test processes, not anything that bled. Had blood. Normal corpses didn't bleed. Rocío wasn't sure about MMF corpses. They might do anything at all.

"You see the problem right?" Yaco said a few moments later, waving a pair of tweezers. Thank the seres celestiales it was clean so Rocío didn't have to dodge fairy bits flung off its tip.

"Of course," Hala said.

"Can someone explain it to me?" Rocío asked, rubbing the scars on her hands.

"It would help if you looked," Hala said without raising her head.

"I don't think so." It wasn't just the open chest cavity of the dead body that disturbed Rocío, it was also the fact that it was an MMF, here.

Yaco put down the tweezers and reached to pull on one bushy black eyebrow. The automatic gesture was foiled by the hair net he'd pulled down low across his forehead for just that reason. Instead he shuffled his feet and cleared his throat. "It seems the body is decomposing from the outside in." He paused expectantly.

"Hmm." Hala bent closer to the dead thing.

"That's not normal?" Rocío asked when neither of them said anything else.

Hala shook her head at her.

"Uh, no. A human body decays from the inside out," Yaco

explained. "With the heart no longer pumping, the blood no longer supplies oxygen, resulting in chemical changes, the release of enzymes at the cellular level and the proliferation of anaerobic bacteria that begin to break down tissue ..." He caught the disgusted expression on Rocío's face and thought better of his pontification on putrefaction and stopped. "No, it's not normal."

"But what does that mean?" Rocío held up a hand to stem another explanation. "Not the part about chemical changes, the part about decaying the wrong way."

"I don't know!" He threw up his hands.

"Hala?"

"We don't know enough about fairy physiology to know if it's normal. You would expect to see this pattern of decay on a corpse that was frozen"—she gestured up, presumably to the hot summer sky—"but what is normal for a magically created and enhanced fairy?"

"Made of magic, I don't think enhanced is the right terminology," Yaco said.

Hala shrugged, conceding the point. "If we don't know what's normal, we don't know what's abnormal. Is this an anomaly to be pursued that could lead to evidence? Or is it normal and therefore of no evidentiary use at all?"

"Oh." Rocío ran through some facial exercises to think. It wasn't something she would do in front of just anyone because it did look odd to the unaccustomed, but Yaco and Hala knew her well enough to not be distracted. "What about the professor who helped with the MMFs?"

"Gone to Enkladt to study," Hala said.

"If this had happened six months in the future we'd have the answers already," Yaco said.

"In more ways than one," Hala said.

"Is there anyone else?" Rocío asked.

Hala and Yaco exchanged a look.

"What? What do you know that I don't?"

"Many things," Hala intoned, the light off her spectacles hiding her eyes.

"Stop equivocating," Rocío said.

"Oh, how the tables have turned," Hala said, clearly referring to Rocío's avoidance of questions relating to her parents, and paused to let that barb sink into its target.

Rocío stuck her tongue out at her.

"It's not the future, so we have to use the resources available to us now." Hala removed her spectacles and raised her eyebrows at Rocío.

Rocío started to get an inkling of where Hala was going with this conversation and why she was taking the roundabout route. Unless Rocío found a way out of it, her immediate future was going to involve sweet talking people she didn't want to talk to and who didn't want to talk to her. Also a trip to the Central Municipal Police. Better known by its acronym, Cempol, or officers of the law who considered themselves the high-and-mighty elites in La Bene. If the professor studying the MMFs wasn't available, the Cempol tech who'd worked with her in November would be the next best thing. The only problem was, Cempol didn't willingly share information with its supposed sister agencies, the community justice centers.

Did Hala suspect it would come to this when she got me pastries? Were they an attempt to butter me up? Literally?

"You found out the name of the forensic tech?" Rocío asked hopefully.

Cempol hadn't shared any information about the MMFs, and as far as Rocío knew, the only thing Miraflores had was the tech's license number, 856080. The list of license numbers was available to the public, but as it was buried deep under multiple layers of bureaucracy guarded by one Yelena Dhavale Cruz, secretary to the Commander of Cempol, officious defender of order, as she defined it, it might as well be in the Ya Empire.

"No," Hala said.

Rocío rubbed the space between her eyebrows. "So we ask Fede to ask her for the name that goes with the license number." Sometimes the indirect route was the most direct, when dealing with interagency politics and most especially bureaucrats, who defended their domains like rams in mating season, except all the time.

Their coworker Detective Federico Dhavale Cruz was the nephew of both the Commander of Cempol and Yelena Dhavale Cruz, arguably the second most powerful person at Cempol. Fede was deployed strategically in emergency situations to cajole her to broader minded action. She doted on him; possibly he was the only person in her life that she loved, and bureaucratic red tape dissolved like soap bubbles in a tidal wave when he asked.

Fede liked Rocío, really liked her; she tried not to trade on that or step on any boundaries that would make her feel icky, but this was not an frivolous request, with MMFs in the picture again, and he liked his aunt, against all reason, so...

"Fede is unavailable," Hala said.

Ah. "So we wait until he is," Rocío said reasonably. Somehow she didn't think that was the conclusion Hala had arrived at.

"Unavailable for several days. Oshinsky sent him to Kooja Ya."

"Why did she do that?" Rocío felt like she was being mercilessly herded. Really, just because she could sometimes talk some people into doing things didn't mean she could talk *everyone* into *anything*. Yelena Dhavale was the proverbial insurmountable obstacle and Rocío had bruised herself on the woman's rigidity before.

"That's immaterial," Hala said.

"Not to me."

"You'll have to do it."

Yaco's head was bobbing back and forth as if he were watching a volley in a fast-paced tennis match.

"Why don't you do it?" Rocío asked him.

"Me? I can't talk an anarchist into bombing a government building."

Rocío sighed. "She won't talk to me at all, Hala," she said, drawing herself up with dignity. "It shouldn't be me." *It's so going to be me.*

"Did you sleep with her?" Yaco asked with all the fascination some people exhibited at fatal vehicle crashes.

Rocío shuddered. "I thought you knew me better than that. We've been friends for how long? That would be like making love to a pneumatic tube. I'm starting to worry about you, Yaco," she said, seizing on this distraction. "You do know that sex is best when both parties are equally enthusiastic? Although if you're thinking of

85

finding an older woman to be your lover, your instincts aren't all wrong—"

"Stop, please. I'm sorry, okay?"

"You started it," Rocío said mildly, her annoyance already evaporating in the face of the bigger problem. Surely there was another way to get this information?

Yaco raised his hands in a fending off gesture. "I'm sorry. I won't mention your sex life again."

"Unlikely," Hala commented. "Everyone talks about Rocío's sex life."

Rocío ignored her. "And I won't talk about yours. No. I told her form F248b wasn't used to request inter-agency personnel cooperation."

"Are you kidding?" Yaco exclaimed.

"Would I kid about form F248b? Also, I might have made things worse."

"How could you have made it worse? You told the most bureaucratic bureaucrat she didn't know how to bureaucrat."

Hala raised an eyebrow at her.

"I gave her a puppy," Rocío admitted. She didn't usually misjudge people so badly, but the fallout from puppygate had been spectacular. And not in a fireworks and balloons kind of spectacular. Metaphorical guts on the floor spectacular; Rocío's guts. "I learned some new swear words though. Hala, you know all this. I can't be the one to talk to her." She looked at Yaco.

"Oh no." He backed away with his hands up. "She'd smash me like an egg in a force test."

"That bad?" Rocío asked. "I think you're underestimating yourself."

"I'm just a magic and science geek. Make Hala do it."

"Yelena doesn't like immigrants." Rocío couldn't think of anyone else who would both stand up to Yelena and not antagonize her into uselessness. And who was flexible enough to deploy extra-alternate methods if needed. Alternate methods were always needed for Yelena.

"Hala's not an immigrant," Yaco cried, reversing course to stab an outraged finger at Rocío.

"My father is." Hala shrugged.

"Don't worry," Rocío said, "I'd sacrifice Yaco on the desk of bureaucratic power hoarding, but that would be too cruel to you, Hala."

"I appreciate the sentiment." The muscles around Hala's eyes relaxed as she accepted Rocío's surrender.

"I..." Yaco looked back and forth between them.

Rocío pensively searched through her pockets and came up empty. Yaco pointed at a drawer to her left. Opened, it revealed a fresh pack of gum. "You're a gem. I wouldn't really sacrifice you, Yaco. We need you here." Rocío popped a fresh stick in her mouth. "This requires... doughnuts. But that's not enough..." Her mind started spinning through options to please a bitter old woman who loved to exert power over others.

"Doughnuts?" Yaco asked.

"Bribes," Rocío said absently.

"Not bribes," Hala said, frowning. "Appeasement."

"Bribes, Hala," Rocío said. "Call it what it is."

"It's not bribery if you're trying to induce someone to do the job they are employed to do. And Rocío." Hala waited until she had Rocío's full attention. "Be more judicious this time."

"Time will tell." She still wasn't sure the puppy had been a mistake, although it certainly looked like one.

Decision made, she hopped down from the counter. "I have to see a man. And I have to change." She looked down at her light cotton huiple, embroidered with flowers considered appropriate for women's wear, and loose trousers.

"Change?" Yaco asked.

"Yelena is one of those women who doesn't like other women." At his puzzled look, she added, "It helps to de-emphasize the feminine when talking to her. Attention to detail, as Hala would say, might get me somewhere. Are you sure you don't want to go, Yaco?"

"I have some coprolites to categorize."

"I don't know what that is, but it sounds fun?"

"Fossilized feces," Hala supplied. "You're going now?"

"I have preparations to make," Rocío said cheerfully, now that her decision was made. She did love a challenge. And if this was the beginning of a slippery slope to doom, well, she'd embrace that too.

"Rocío."

"I'll tell you if it works." *Because it's a long shot.*

CHAPTER 10

IT WASN'T that easy to get away from a case of suspected bioterrorism, however, even with Hala's help. Rocío had to review and sign off on yesterday's reports and witness statements and at least skim through a stack of other official paperwork: the cargo manifest for Costas's boat and trading license, a list of the crew members and their children, half of whom had the name of the boat, Resolute, as their sole surname. The other half had the surname Buscadorx, Hogar or Aventura. The discovery that the second mate's name was Buenaventura Aventura made her smile.

Rocío also flipped through the expired marriage contracts for Costas and Pilar, both to Benerex men, one named Ruben Biel Páez and the other Ariano Serafini Verdugo, with parental responsibilities in Pilar's name, for her children, and no children listed on Costas's. Pilar's little girl, Eloisa Constante, had been born in La Bene four years ago. There was no record for the boy, so he had probably been born in the Ya Empire. Nothing unusual about that, the way the river folk traveled.

The two reports Rocío wanted to see, that Pilar had been located and Costas had regained consciousness did not show up. It was a bad sign that Doctor Andrade had not contacted them. She stuck the last report in the folder and handed it across to Hala, who was frowning at the list of dead and injured from November's attack. Rocío squeezed Hala's shoulder. "Okay if I go?"

"Hmm?" Hala lifted her head, blinking her eyes into focus. "You're still here?"

"I'm trying to leave now."

Hala pushed her spectacles onto her head and pinched the top of her nose, though Rocío didn't think it was eyestrain she was trying to get rid of. Three months wasn't enough time. Rocío's body still clenched up when she had to read those lists, with familiar names, including her own. She always had a headache after, from refusing to cry, again.

"Yes, of course." Hala clasped Rocío's hand for a moment, offering and accepting comfort. Some people thought Hala was distant, but it was only that casual touches affected her more and so she limited them to the people who understood that.

After that, Rocío finally hurried home, but it was already afternoon by the time she stepped out of her apartment building, now dressed in a huiple with masculine-appropriate flowers, a breast band that de-emphasized said attributes, slightly wider loose tan trousers, and hairpins topped with polished amethyst-colored glass beads, also coded masculine. She wasn't trying to pass for a man, merely downplaying her womanliness to try to bypass Yelena Dhavale's instinctive distaste.

The sun blazed down from directly overhead so that even the shadows seemed to hide. The heat lay over the afternoon like a blanket, making Rocío feel like melting into the cobblestones and never moving again. Instead, she turned left and mentally reviewed her plan. In spite of what she'd said to Hala and Yaco earlier, she needed something more in hand than doughnuts to get on Yelena Dhavale's good side after the F248b-puppy mistake. It said a lot about Yelena Dhavale's grudging nature that everyone, including Rocío, thought she was the best chance to get what they needed from her. She was an avid opera fan and Rocío happened to know—only because Fede Dhavale had said so—that she had purchased season tickets this year for the Andretti Opera, as usual, but then Monserrat Renata Bartoli, La Bene's premier opera singer and Yelena Dhavale's favorite, had made her surprise announcement that she would be performing at the Academy of Music instead. And Yelena still did not have tickets. The problem was Rocío didn't have tickets either.

"Detective Rocío!"

A chaski huffed up, flushed and wet with sweat, flourishing an envelope. Heat seemed to come off her in waves, rivaling those radiating from the stone buildings and street.

Rocío drew her into the shade of a sapote tree after a quick scan to assure herself none of the fruits were positioned to fall on their heads. "What's this?"

"A message from your parents! I went to the CJC first, and they told me to try to find you here, but now it's late! They told me it was time sensitive!"

Oh no. I never thanked them for the dress. Her heart clenched and she almost raised her hand to her chest, but the chaski was watching and would repeat anything for spare change. *How could I have forgotten? MMFs, bioterrorism, abused advocates, your job,* the logical part of her mind listed. As if any of that would matter to her parents.

"Don't worry about it." Rocío thought her voice sounded normal enough that the chaski hadn't noticed her reaction. "Ask my concierge for water." She pointed the chaski in the right direction and helped her on her way with a push between the shoulders towards the open door.

Rocío turned the envelope over in her hands, looking, not for clues to its contents, but to the mystery of her parents. It had taken a long time—years after escaping her childhood home—for Rocío to realize that most parents did not act as if their children were extensions of themselves, that the good ones in fact celebrated equally the differences, similarities and achievements of their children. Rocío had asked her nonna, once, what was wrong with her parents and if it was because they had no living siblings. Nonna was normal. But Nonna hadn't answered.

Rocío went to the far side of the tree and opened the message. It was an invitation to lunch, but it was on stationary from Constanza's, the banquet hall where her parents were celebrating their contract signing, and apparently doing a menu tasting for the party, which meant they had sent it after they arrived and Rocío would have been late even if the chaski hadn't had to chase her all over the neighborhood. *So this is my punishment. The start of it, anyway.*

She crumpled the letter in her fist, a small act of defiance that gave her more relief from her feelings than she thought it should, and stared unseeing at the street. She had to go bribe a government official. But if she went to see her parents now, they might possibly forgive her before their party, which would be easier for her. Who was she kidding? She would never hear the end of it from them, either way. But it would be worse if she didn't go now. She kicked one of the fallen sapotes into the side of the building with a satisfying thwack.

Her stomach rumbled at the scent of bruised, over-ripe fruit. She'd been planning on skipping lunch and trying to wheedle a favor from a friend who worked at the Academy of Music. But her parents were offering lunch, and she needed to appease them.

They were also avid opera fans.

So, new plan, and maybe she'd accomplish three things at once.

Stepping into Constanza's felt like stepping out of summer. The stone walls held back the heat and a slight current of cool air teased the hems of Rocío's trousers and her huiple, although as many times as she had been here she had never spotted the hidden source. Of course, there was usually something else to keep her attention; it was popular for celebrating wedding contracts and charity dinners. Although the hall—there was no other name for the wide expanse of floor and the vaulted ceilings arching three stories above—was reasonably full with diners and waitstaff and tables, it was hushed and restrained. Constanza's was one of the rare luxury venues that made the transition to lunch service without looking tawdry and overdone.

The maitre d' noticed her and after a quick word led Rocío to her parents.

From the lack of dishes on the table, it seemed she wasn't too late after all.

"Rocío, really, how can you stand to be seen in those clothes?" Her father sniffed. He stood, leading with his paunch, projecting a kind of smug certainty. Xavier whuffled through his thick mustache as they exchanged fake kisses. He smelled of old-fashioned cologne, a hint of cloves and cassia.

She glanced down, even though she knew perfectly well what she had chosen to wear, and it was respectable, well-made clothing, just not designer or even tailor-made. "I'm dressed for work."

"Don't be ridiculous, Rocío." Her mother presented her cheek, and Rocío exchanged air kisses with her.

Analicía always seemed sleek and a little brittle to Rocío, as if her tight gestures, the expensive dye hiding the gray in her hair and the designer clothes held her together. The image was deceptive on both levels: the facade didn't extend over her worst behaviors and Rocío had seen her mother shout and cry for hours without rest. Rocío and her mother had the same square face and height, but inside they were nothing alike. Both Rocío's parents were in their sixties, though you'd have to look closely to guess.

"Never mind, at least you have something decent to wear for the party," her mother said. "You received the dress?" She didn't wait for Rocío's reply. "Aurelian charged exorbitantly for the lace and it took forever to get the satin ribbons, but it will be worth it because Yara's daughter tried to get them for her dress but I made that impossible." She held up a triumphant hand, signaling for the waiter.

Rocío couldn't remember who Yara and her daughter was and certainly didn't care about Analicía's feuds, but that meant the dress wasn't just a dress to her mother. Not that it ever was. Rocío hid her grimace by unfolding her napkin in her lap. She always meant to be firm, to state her desires clearly and ignore her parents. But that always seemed easier when she wasn't with them. And Analicía had that sharp look today, like anything would push her over the edge, even in public. It was always easier to avoid her parents than confront them. The disappointment in herself was a too-familiar emotion. She wished she hadn't come.

"Where are Miguel and Sebastián?" she said, asking after her brother and his spouse.

"Don't be silly darling, they're at work."

And I'm not? Rocío gritted her teeth on her response and was saved by a fastidious waiter with a graying mustache appearing at their table with a tray of ... cake. Rocío's stomach grumbled, reminding her of how long ago breakfast had been.

She turned to her father, unable to speak to her mother for the moment. "Your note said lunch. That's not lunch. I thought we were here to decide on the menu for your party."

"This is the cake tasting," her father said. "We had lunch without you." He'd dyed his hair again recently, for not even a hint of grey showed at the roots, and the new hairpins, tipped with matching star sapphires, glimmered with the light as he made his pronouncement.

Rocío sucked in a breath. So this was her punishment for not fawning over them for the dress. She looked away from her parents' avid expressions and met the waiter's eyes. His face was completely blank of expression, but she thought she saw sympathy in his eyes, and she blushed that he was witnessing her humiliation.

"Thank you for the dress," she said mechanically. "I'm sorry to have been so gauche as to not say so immediately."

"Oh, no, darling, we planned it that way." Her mother gestured at the waiter.

He selected one of the offerings and displayed it. "This is the traditional thousand layer cake with dulce de leche but as you can see the frosting is..."

Rocío tuned him out, breathing deeply to regain her equilibrium. Her options were to leave and never hear the end of it; stay, suffer through and hope that was enough for them and that she could get opera tickets out of them; or pay Constanza's outrageous prices for lunch. Or...

The waiter centered the last plate of delicate cake on the table and Rocío plunged into the conversational hole.

"Señorx, if you please, I'll have the sirloin, medium rare, cucumber salad and provoleta, at my parents' invitation."

"Of course, detective. I'll leave you to your discussion." The waiter's eyelid fluttered in a quick wink behind her mother's back. She just hoped he hadn't sneezed—or worse—on any of the food before serving, though she wouldn't blame him if he had. Her parents had never grasped that the people who served them had great power over them at the same time.

"Really, darling, you're going to have steak while we eat cake?" her mother said.

Rocío took guilty pleasure in the forced quality of her words. "Oh no, I'm going to eat cake while you eat cake. Though I think you should have alfajores instead of cake." The dulce de leche sandwich cookies were sold on every street corner of La Bene. Not that that made them less delicious. "They're always a crowd pleaser."

"Oh, Rocío, you can't be serious. I don't think Constanza's would even have alfajores on the menu."

"No mother, of course not. And I want to spend time with you,"—she'd been an actor long before she left her parents house and going on stage just meant she got applause for it—"and if I have to eat steak while you eat cake, that's a sacrifice I'm willing to make. What is this about Yara and her daughter?"

That was enough to set Analicía off on a running monologue about her rivalry, interspersed with comments from Xavier about the superiority of Constanza's cuisine and the difficulties with fabric imports, that lasted until Rocío's steak arrived.

The steak settled her stomach and her emotions better than the cake, and Rocío decided on her gambit. It wouldn't do to come at it too directly though. She let her parents conversation—and sniping—pass over her, if not with ease, then with the familiarity of practice, waiting for her opening. It came when her father mentioned a business connection who was rapidly solidifying his fortune through mineral exploitation and entering that sphere of society Rocío personally dubbed rich enough for everyone to ignore his family's lack of connections to the leading families of La Bene. "I heard he secured season tickets for the opera performances at the Academy of Music and that it's been quite a challenge this year."

Her parents didn't approve of Rocío having been in the arts—in their opinion their status required them to be patrons, who enjoyed from a safe distance the slightly out of kilterness of the people who created art. That Rocío had been an actor cast a certain doubt on the... wholesomeness... of her family in her parents' view, an opinion shared by those closest to them on the social ladder of La Bene. Rocío wasn't sure if those at the top shared the sentiment; politics after all was performance, and required a similarly altered perception of reality to produce: an ego big enough to present itself for consumption by an audience, narrow focus and a slantwise relationship to the truth.

"Oh, no, of course we didn't have any problems, those difficulties are not for our sort, Rocío, which you'd know if you ever paid attention to anything I ever told you."

Rocío had to head that off before her lack of ambition and dutiful feelings became the topic of conversation. Really, you'd think her brother's exclusive marriage contract for the next seven years and the high class surname coming out of that for his two children would be enough for her parents, but it never was.

"Of course, mother, you're right," Rocío said.

Her mother preened.

"I also heard he gave tickets to Commander Dhavale's secretary for the Andretti Opera. Of course everyone knows she will give them to the commander. But his favorite performer is Monserrat Renata Bartoli and she's only at the Academy of Music this season."

There. She'd dangled the bait, now she needed to let her parents swim into the net themselves.

Commander Dhavale really did like opera, though Rocío had never heard that he had a favorite performer. The Dhavale family was a relative newcomer to La Bene, arriving only a century ago, but they had intermarried and inter-fecundated with the leading families, including the Montenegros, O'Higgins, Sotos and Cruces, to be included among the city's elite and influential and her parents' list of people they wanted to socialize with.

Her parents exchanged looks. The waiter arrived with perfect timing and another assortment of cakes. Rocío agreed that the creme liqueurs were too heavy for a summer party, and waited. "What about white cake? It's simple and understated. It should go well with...wait, you never did tell me the main menu."

"Four suckling pigs and a roast swan," her father said absently, eyes on her mother's.

Rocío choked on her bite of cake.

"Swan?" She gulped water. "I didn't think Constanza's had swan on the menu."

"They don't dear; they're doing it special for us. We wanted the grandeur of an old banquet."

And that was really more than Rocío could stand for the day, not and have any emotional bandwidth to also deal with Yelena Dhavale. Though at least Yelena didn't hide her feelings.

She'd given them enough time to think about it. Time to bring the fishies into the net.

She placed her napkin on the table and pushed back her chair. "I must be going."

"Now, darling, you haven't tried any of the chocolate mousse cake."

Rocío let them cajole her for a few minutes, leaning back in her chair and letting the exasperation they expected to show on her face. "Mother," she said finally, standing up. "I have an important appointment at Cempol, it's work. You wouldn't be interested."

"With Commander Dhavale?" her father asked.

Rocío bit her lip, pretending reluctance. "How—you know I can't tell you that."

Her father smiled complacently through his mustache and folded his hands on his stomach.

"I've told you before that a lot of my work is confidential. But you see I really must go." *Come on. Do what comes so naturally to you.*

"Wait, darling." Analicía detained Rocío with a cool hand on hers.

Excitement buzzed through Rocío. She turned it into a pained smile.

"So much of your *job* is busy work, but meeting with Commander Dhavale, now that's something we can be proud of."

Somehow that pride never included Rocío, but managed to exclude her from the very things she was doing.

"Do you think you could manage a little gift for him?" Analicía wheedled.

"Mother! No."

"We can't let these parvenus outdo us, darling, try to understand."

"Good-bye, mother, father." Rocío bent to kiss her mother.

Analicía turned her shoulder to Rocío, and Rocío drew back, her acting forgotten in that simple act of rejection. *They always win, even when I'm winning.*

"Why can't she understand?" Analicía cried to Xavier.

"You're upsetting your mother," Xavier said with exaggerated patience. Rocío really had not inherited her acting skills from him. "You wouldn't have to say they're from us. You could just hint."

Rocío shrugged choppily. "Fine, fine. What a waste of time." Some of her real pain seeped into her voice. *It's all verisimilitude. Just use it.* "I suppose you want me to pick them up, too."

"Oh, darling, maybe you do understand."

"That just makes her lack of understanding for other things more egregious." Her father frowned, making his mustache bristle. "Here, give this to Giovanni at the Academy of Music." He extracted a leather wallet holding his monogrammed stationary from his bag, scribbled a note and scrawled his signature on it.

"This has been," *upsetting, ostentatious, rude,* "a *lovely* interlude, but I must go."

She disentangled herself from her mother's grip. As she walked away, her parents cooed at each other in self satisfaction. They had no idea Rocío had *won* that round.

Tickets to bribe Yelena Dhavale, not only free of charge, but free of *obligation* to her parents because they thought they had manipulated her, rather than the other way around. This might even cut short the punishment they'd normally extract for the lack of gratitude for the dress—her mother carried a grudge forever—but now they thought she was acting as a daughter should, advancing their agenda and serving their needs. They were practically in her debt. Not that they would see it that way.

She knew that her acting and her ability to persuade people came from a tainted source she didn't want to examine too closely, but it felt good to wield them against her parents. It was a win-win-win situation. She felt like she won, her parents felt like they won, and Yelena Dhavale was about to win the opera lottery. Rocío was practically bouncing by the time she reached the door.

She found the manager and praised the waiter's service and discretion, which wasn't nearly enough compensation for putting up with her parents, making sure the waiter could hear too. And then she slipped the waiter five pesos, an extravagant tip even for Constanza's. His reading of her signals had been admirable.

CHAPTER 11

BUOYED by her triumph with her parents, she wasn't even worried about Yelena Dhavale and enjoyed her walk. She felt a grim sort of pride that she was smart enough to use her parents' fixations for something worthwhile and that she could survive them, and therefore anything Yelena could do to her. After all, as a bureaucrat, she only had the power of life and death over Rocío in limited intervals, while her parents had meddled with Rocío's psyche over a lifetime.

She picked up the tickets, and doughnuts at Yelena's favorite bakery, without a problem and then cut through the plaza at the heart of La Bene to Cempol's offices. Although the Miraflores CJC was only a few blocks from the Plaza de la ciudad, the neighborhood couldn't be more different.

The five-sided Plaza was an enormous expanse of stone pavers, capable of holding a hundred thousand people at a time, dominated on one side by the seat of government, the House of Refuges, and at the other by a stone amphitheater. Now that it was no longer blanketed in the summer fair, it felt almost empty in spite of groups of musicians and their audiences, kids flying a yellow and blue kite, and vendors selling everything from shaved ice to tablecloths in the style called La Bene lace, which wasn't lace at all but cutwork with traditional patterns of knots connecting across the empty spaces. The guitarist and violinist were good. Wanting to spread her good feeling, she dropped a peso in the guitar case as she passed.

In accordance with the logic of bureaucratic hierarchy, Commander Dhavale's, and thus his secretary's, office was deep in a labyrinth of offices and meeting rooms, requiring the twelve labors of a mythic hero to reach. However, the commander also valued his ability to quickly escape—that is, appear where needed—so there was a side door. Rocío circumvented the alarm with a little spurt of magic. It was a safety regulation, intended to warn the occupants of an emergency requiring speedy egress, not a security measure, so she didn't feel bad about it, and it allowed her to appear in Yelena's doorway without having to use up all her patience on employees who couldn't, and didn't want to, give her what she wanted.

She leaned in the doorway, observing Yelena for a moment. She didn't look like the terror of Cempol. With her face in repose, the wrinkles around her mouth and eyes were merely a sign of age, not fierce displeasure or possibly dyspepsia (it was one possible explanation for why she was so unpleasant; stomach problems were enough to make anyone rude). The pins in her graying hair were tasteful, her Iberex style suit outdated but of good quality, and her fine-boned hands relaxed as she flipped through the pages of some report.

Something prompted Yelena to look up. The mouth and wrinkles drew up in a snarl and the hands tightened so that the tendons stood up on their backs. She slapped the report closed.

"What are you doing here?"

Smiling, Rocío displayed the doughnut box with a flourish, the pink and white script immediately recognizable to anyone in the know.

"Are you trying to bribe me?" Yelena asked. Her tone made it clear that anyone daring such a misadventure would get the fate they deserved, but she couldn't hide her avaricious glance at the box. To cover it, she snapped, "Or is this a transparent effort at social climbing?"

That stung, more than it usually would, fresh off the lunch with her parents, but then the old woman's barbs usually did. Her aim was almost always unerring. La Bene was small enough that all the rich elite knew each other and knew who was trying to join their ranks. Of course Yelena knew about Rocío's parents; as a bureaucrat and a politician, her currency was information and Rocío had drawn her notice with the F248b puppy.

"You'll never satisfy them you know." Yelena's lips bent in a simulacrum of a smile.

Rocío's own pleasant expression slipped, and Yelena's smile became real. To cover her mistake, Rocío said, "Yelena, I didn't know you cared. You're keeping tabs on me and my parents these days, are you?" She needed to redirect the conversation, quickly. "You say bribe, I say apology." She put her hand over her heart dramatically.

Yelena's expression returned to bitter. Rocío was glad for the final gleaming barrier of Yelena's desk. It would make it harder for an old lady to murder her. Or for her to murder the old lady. Now that Rocío was in Yelena's office, she had some sympathy; the overpowering decorations in Cempol crimson, purple, royal blue and gold would drive Rocío to bitterness and murder, too.

"A petition to get back into your good graces so that you might again extend to me a professional courtesy that you would to any officer of the law." Bureaucrats and snobs liked to have their egos stroked and Yelena was both, while it cost Rocío nothing. Besides she enjoyed the chance to ham it up; comedies had been so fun to act in. There was so little chance she'd succeed, after all.

Yelena eyed her narrowly, not allowing her eyes to drop to the temptation in Rocío's hands.

Clearly sterner measures were called for.

First, Rocío stated the obvious. "The doughnuts are from Diana's." A favored bakery not close enough to the offices for a daytime trip from the office to be feasible. "Passion fruit frosting." Yelena's favorite. Fede had mentioned it in passing one day.

Rocío flipped the lid open, letting out the smells of fried dough, sugar and passionfruit, and tipped the box so Yelena could see the six plump doughnuts slathered with pale yellow frosting. "With chocolate nibs."

Yelena's eyes narrowed even more but they dropped to the box and she swallowed. "Give them to me," she said, folding her hands on the desk.

Rocío rather thought that was an aborted grab. Ceremoniously, she placed them within Yelena's reach with the lid still open.

"Now go away, I'll think about it." Yelena smiled maliciously.

Rocío settled on the arm of one the chairs facing the desk. "Ah, but I have something else I know you want, and you'll have to talk to me to get it."

"There is nothing you have that I want. You gave me a *dog,* ancestros protect you, because you're going to need it in this life. Go away and—"

"Two tickets to see Monserrat Renata Bartoli on the first night she performs at the Academy of Music." Rocío reached into her pocket and retrieved the tickets. She fanned them so Yelena could see them clearly.

Yelena stopped with her mouth open. Her hands twitched. She swallowed.

The trick was to prevent Yelena from saying anything she couldn't go back on. Which mostly meant not letting her talk.

Rocío knew other people complained that people should do their jobs, and that was true, but people were complex, conflicted, petty, generous, and motivated by a whole range of things that most often had nothing to do with their jobs. And Rocío enjoyed finding the lever that moved people. She didn't think it was much different from, for example, knowing what form of affection your lover responded best to. Khaled was all about physical affection, while Isis responded to words. Hala—not her lover but her closest friend—could be left speechless with the right gift, one that said, "I know you and see you." Rocío was quite smug Hala still hadn't mastered the Jeen puzzle box she had given her at the end of the year—the earrings in the secret compartment hadn't yet made an appearance.

"Let's see." Rocío made a show of examining the tickets. "Section D, seats A25 and A26. Those are very good seats in the orchestra level, aren't they?" She tapped one. "And look at the date. Friday, 6 March. In just over a month from now you could be sitting in the darkened theater, waiting for that first ecstatic note to caress your ears and thrum through your skin." Yelena was very sensitive to textures as well as sound, Rocío had noticed. The linen in her suit was mixed with a high percentage of cotton, softening it, she used pins with nubbed ends in her hair, and the hangings in her office did a good job of muffling noise, which would otherwise bounce off the hard walls.

"I don't know why you think I would be interested." Yelena's chin rose so she could look down her nose at Rocío. It was a good trick, since her head was lower.

If Rocío drew this out, Yelena would interpret it as a taunt, that Rocío never intended to hand over the tickets. Besides it wouldn't do to enjoy this too much; that was probably bad for her soul.

"And all you have to do is give me the name that goes with the license number of the tech that worked on the MMFs last year with the professor," Rocío said briskly. "You get to help the city again, and you get a little something for yourself. You deserve that, don't you?"

Yelena transferred her gaze to Rocío's face. *Oops. maybe that was laying it on too thick?* She ran her thumb over the edge of one ticket.

Yelena opened the top drawer and extracted a ledger, and Rocío knew she had won.

Forensic tech, license number 856080, Trinidad Fonseca Enriquez, assistant to the absent local expert on MMFs, and the object of most of Rocío's emotional and psychological wrangling today, was boiling something that smelled very bad.

From the doorway, Rocío got the impression of a tall, gangling figure before one long arm reached out, swept up an empty beaker and hurled it at her.

She stepped aside and it shattered against the far wall. A piece of glass landed on her sandaled foot and glittered in the strong lighting Cempol favored in the lower levels where forensic staff worked.

"I said get out and I meant it," an irate voice informed her.

Rocío shook the glass off her foot. "You must be popular with the cleaning staff. Do they rearrange all your equipment at night?" She stepped back into the doorway.

A young woman with the most remarkable—and surprising—coloring scowled at Rocío, the bright blue of her eyes fierce against the rich brown of her skin. Her dark red hair curled tightly to her head, a color Rocío couldn't remember seeing before, especially on someone with such a Benerex name. People in La Bene tended to brown hair, brown eyes and medium brown skin, like Rocío herself.

"Are you Trinidad Fonseca Enriquez?" Rocío asked.

"If I say yes, you're not going to go away, are you?"

"License number 856080?" Rocío felt bad for asking again as soon as the words were out of her mouth. The power of expectations was like gravity, fine for walking around keeping your feet grounded on the planet, dangerous if you stepped off a cliff, insulting when you made assumptions.

"Can't you read? Or did you fail basic schooling and that's why you're on the janitorial staff?" Trinidad stalked across the room with a long-legged stride that ate up the ground between them.

Rocío wondered what Trinidad thought she was going to do when she got to her. "Read what?"

"Read what!" Trinidad stabbed a finger at the door and then her mouth gaped open. "There was a sign!" she howled. "Perdidos block-heads. That does it, get out, get out."

Trinidad seized Rocío's arm and tried to strong-arm her out the door.

Rocío's patience snapped. She'd been planning to appeal to Trinidad's scholarly curiosity—the woman who'd written the reports on the MMFs had to have it—but an attempt at manhandling was too much. Rocío shifted her weight to the side. As Trinidad's own momentum kept her moving forward, Rocío captured her thumb and, using the leverage of tendons and joints, twisted her arm up behind her back. It worked just as well on irascible scientists as it did on drunks.

"What!" Trinidad struggled against Rocío's grip and then went limp as that ground her tendons against bone. "Let go. You can't do this. I'm in the middle of an important investigation. They need my test results—"

"I can. Yelena Dhavale told me where to find you."

Trinidad went completely limp and Rocío had to let go to avoid seriously injuring the young woman. Those amazing eyes widened in panic and she swallowed. "She did?"

"I suggest you turn off your burner because you're coming with me. And you'd better figure out a way to apologize to the cleaning staff for the mess you're leaving or you'll have worse to deal with than figuring out where they hid your microscopes."

Trinidad scuttled away, doing as she said, and by the time she returned Rocío's annoyance had died down enough to introduce herself. "Let's go. I'm Detective Rocío Díaz Rossi from—"

"—from Miraflores CJC? Why didn't you say so?" Trinidad gaped at her in horrified dismay.

"You didn't give me—"

"I threw a beaker at you! I didn't know! It was one of my new beakers, you know. If that helps. Why didn't you say so? I wouldn't have thrown a beaker at *you*. I've been wanting to talk to you about the MMFs but I wasn't sure—the CJCs and Cempol don't always get along but now you're here talking to me. Why didn't you say immediately who you are?"

Rocío waited a beat to see if Trinidad was done talking. "I didn't have a chance," she said dryly. "And maybe you shouldn't throw beakers at people. And have you considered that insulting people by calling them cleaning staff says more about you than them?"

Trinidad hunched her shoulders and mumbled something Rocío didn't catch. Well, that was a relief. She'd thought maybe Trinidad only had one volume: loud; which would have made a circumspect conversation about MMFs difficult.

CHAPTER 12

Trinidad looked around the lab-turned-autopsy, spotted the MMF and made a beeline for it. Humming deep in her throat, she circled the table, examining the corpse from all angles with the naked eye and then repeated her circuit, this time using the magnifying glasses. Yaco followed, copying her, as if by sheer will he could see the MMF the way she did. As she faced Rocío, one disturbing blue eye appeared behind a lens, distorted and wavy at this magnification, the color of the iris visible like threads. Trinidad blinked, and the pupil dilated, swallowing the brightness.

Rocío boosted herself on the counter again, this time with the double aim of distancing herself from the cadaver and whatever Trinidad had to say. With a glance that measured Rocío's distance, Hala stationed herself at the head of the improvised autopsy table.

"Ooh, this one isn't going to last much longer." Trinidad grabbed something pointy and poked at the MMF's extremities. "It's on the verge of dissolving. You can tell by the wingtips, fingers and toes. We need masks and goggles. The fairy dust is toxic when it goes poof."

The cool of the basement and the sweat drying on her back was enough to make Rocío shiver. She rummaged in the drawer for safety gear and handed it out before resuming her perch. The straps on the mask immediately started hurting her ears.

"What does that tell you?" Hala asked, her voice muffled behind her mask.

"No wonder you needed me." Trinidad placed the pointy thing back on the instrument tray with a decisive click and donned her own protective gear. "By itself, it would tell me that this specimen has been in La Bene for at least eight days. Normally by the ninth day they turn completely gray and sometime on the tenth they go poof." Trinidad raised her hand with the fingers and thumb touching and then flicked her fingers open.

"You said normally," Hala said.

"How long have you had it? Under what conditions was it found?"

Hala summarized the location, time of day, and when pressed, the estimated temperature and how long the MMF could have been on the boat without being seen. "We recovered it yesterday. If it was on the boat for eight days, do you think its rate of deterioration might have changed as it crossed national boundaries?"

Trinidad stared through Hala, her eyebrows mashed together in an intense scowl.

"Another variable, Hala?" Yaco asked. "Don't we have enough?"

"You're asking if the MMF was on the boat with Pilar and Costas before they arrived in La Bene?" Rocío asked. "Meaning they brought their trouble with them?"

"It's a possibility we need to consider." Hala shrugged. "In one way, it would be reassuring. A self-contained drama that just happened to play out in our city."

"And in another way, so not reassuring." Yaco waved both hands in a negating gesture. "Viable MMFs in the Ya Empire!"

Abruptly, Trinidad came out of her trance and bent over the MMF again. "I think that's unlikely. You must have noticed the skin slippage and the rapid deterioration of the tissues?"

"Of course. You can see the cellular damage with the stronger microscope." Yaco waved to a table covered in instruments. "But with no baseline for comparison I have no idea if it's normal for MMFs or not. That's why we need you."

Trinidad followed Yaco's wave to the other table and bent to look through the microscope. After a moment she straightened and pinched the shoulders of her huiple to self-importantly adjust the way it lay. "It is absolutely not normal. *Culicidae sapiens* decomposes in the exact same way that Homo sapiens does. The cells do not rupture, and decomposition occurs just as it does for any other animal, from the inside out. Therefore, this MMF was frozen."

"Frozen in the middle of summer?" Hala asked. "It's almost forty Celsius today."

"So you're saying the MMF was stored on ice?" Rocío asked. "That wasn't on the cargo manifest for Pilar's boat."

"That would cause ice burns at the contact points." Yaco scratched at his head through the hair net. His hair was so thick Rocío wondered if his fingers reached his scalp.

"Did you find any physical evidence it had been wrapped?" Trinidad asked.

"No," Yaco said, glaring at the MMF.

"It's not surprising." Hala patted Yaco on the shoulder. "It was outside in a windy and sunny location. Trinidad, we know that imported magic can survive for ten days in La Bene, not including a sea voyage. What happens if imported magic, a MFF for example, were frozen before being brought to La Bene? Or after it arrived here? Could it survive freezing? Would it be alive? Would freezing change the countdown for foreign magic to lose its potency, even form? From ten days to indefinite?"

"Oh dear." Trinidad stared at Hala with wide eyes, and Rocío realized just how young the scientist was. "I don't know. "

"The question hasn't come up before this," Hala said. "It's not your fault you don't know."

"Wait," Rocío said. "Are you saying we don't know how long that thing has been here? Or if it was alive or dead? That it might have been here for eight days, alive? Or that it might have died in November?"

Trinidad bent abruptly back to the table, hiding her expression. "I can't believe you're still using the three thousand series comparison microscope. We've had the forty-five hundred at Cempol for at least two years."

Rocío ignored the disparaging remark, obviously intended to draw attention away from that moment of real fear.

Yaco pulled at his eyebrow and stared into space.

"Yaco? Hala?" Rocío asked when it seemed no one was going to answer.

"From what Trinidad has told us, your understanding of the situation is correct. We don't know how long the MMF has been here, we can only estimate how long it has been here while not being frozen. If being frozen somehow halts the countdown on imported magic. Which we also do not know."

"Okay." Rocío knew better than to fix her hair while in a lab, but she had a strong urge to rake her fingers through it and redo all the pins. "I don't think we can answer that right now. So back to something we can: if the river folk weren't importing ice, does that mean they didn't bring the MMF with them? That it was already here in La Bene?"

Trinidad popped up and spoke rapidly. "I'm not sure ice could create such uniform freezing. Wouldn't there be gaps where part of the MMF wasn't in contact with ice? They store ice in big blocks, right? It's not my area of expertise."

Rocío and Yaco stared at her in surprise. Hala didn't look up, intent on her own thoughts.

"What?" Trinidad said. "It's not a failure to say you don't know something."

"I know that," Rocío said. "I just didn't know you knew that."

"I made a bad impression, I know, but—"

Hala stepped in between them. "Never mind that. I have an idea."

Rocío looked at the business card in her hand again. The thin cardstock was printed with the words "Finn Azimi Ferrar, Inventor, 4 Calle inocentes"—the inventor of the washing machines they'd seen at the summer fair.

Hala's thought process had figuratively taken her from the incongruence of a thoroughly frozen corpse in summer to machines to the idea that one inventor might know if other inventors were working on a device that could defy the summer heat and keep bodies—and other more useful things—cold. And that had taken them literally to this narrow intersection where three streets came together.

Rocío squinted again at the fading sign painted in white and blue on the corner of a building. "Calle central. That's reaching." The alleys, none more than two paces across, lay in a tangle around them. Urban planning, urban renewal and urban surveying had been held back for centuries by the increasingly dense neighborhood. It wasn't a slum, but it was close. The bones of the Ya city preceding La Bene could be seen in the some of the stone buildings, but only just. On top of that were layers of architecture, like a three dimensional history of the immigrants who had lived here. Three-story brick and stucco buildings with leaded, mullioned windows in the Talmen style leaned on a Jeen temple, almost hiding from view the roof corners upturned like the flick of a wrist and a faded mosaic of dragons and flowers.

On Rocío's left, a long, low, windowless building of no discernible provenance slumped at one end, like the ground had settled under it, leaving the rest stranded almost five centimeters higher at the far end. A bird trilled insistently from its eaves. There was no one in sight, but Rocío could smell human activity: laundry soap and steam, potatoes roasting and the sharp hot smell of wood carving. And underneath that...ozone and burnt brown sugar. "I smell magic."

Hala folded a section of her map under. Turning to face the warehouse, she held it up and compared its markings to the reality. "That should be number four. Calle inocentes should be on the far side." She sounded aggrieved about her navigation skills.

"If you're right, you got us close. That map can't be accurate."

Hala went left and Rocío went right, looking for a door. At the corner, Rocío's path was blocked by what looked like the confused offspring of a bicycle and a water mill. She tilted her head, trying to spot a way around it.

"Found it." Hala's voice floated back faintly and Rocío abandoned the new conundrum in favor of the more pressing one.

She had walked almost entirely around the building the other way before she met Hala at an unpainted but newish wooden door. Next to it a shiny brass plaque matched the business card: "Finn Azimi Ferrar, Inventor, 4 Calle inocentes." A matching bell the size of Hala's head hung next to it. It jangled tunefully and loudly when Hala pulled the cord.

They waited.

Hala had just rung it again when the door shuddered open, catching on the uneven lintel, revealing the man with the washing machines from the summer fair. His light brown hair fizzed in an aureole around the pins holding it in place, leather gloves were tucked under one arm and the thick leather apron he wore had a large scorch mark on the front that still reeked of burning. He also smelled of magic.

"Ah! I recognize you! Who are you?" He scratched his chin and dropped the gloves. "Was I expecting you? No, I'd remember that. No, no, I got them." He forestalled Rocío's crouch and gathered up the gloves. "To what do I owe this unexpected pleasure?"

"We thought you might be able to help us," Rocío said.

"Oh, do you need something built? Or maybe fixed?"

"We're here in our official capacity. As detectives from Miraflores CJC," Hala added when he stared at them blankly. "Can we come inside?"

"Official capacity! I'm not sure I realized you had one. Someone hasn't complained about the noise have they? Or no, this isn't Miraflores at all, so it can't be that. The building is in Inés del Bosque. Or Saltamontes. Not even the city registrar's office can decide, so some years I pay no taxes and some years I pay in both districts, which is rather an inconvenience, but don't worry, I set aside money, it's just the principle of the thing, why can't they decide?"

His good natured burbling—not a nervous response, Rocío thought, just a characteristic one—took them through a large, high-ceilinged room with some kind of defunct machinery, through a barred metal wall, with the rusted door stuck in the open position, to the back half of the room, which was obviously his workspace. Wooden and metal tables ranked in orderly files with various bits and pieces or entire machines, and wrenches, screwdrivers, some kind of welder and other more mysterious tools on them. Free-standing bins on wheels clustered around the table closest to them with labels like "1.75 couplings" and "Hex nuts M14 x 2."

"Tea?" He turned a small clock on another table to read its face. "Yes, tea."

"Our questions?" Hala headed him off. "Do you know of a machine that can keep things cold?"

For the first time he looked furtive, glancing up at the ceiling and to the side.

"We don't want proprietary secrets," Rocío rushed to say. "We just want to know who might have one."

He shook his head and studied his gloves. "Nope, no, I can't help you."

He lied badly.

Hala leaned against the table behind her and rubbed her ear. Rocío shook her head, communicating back *You do it*. She thought Hala's enthusiasm would be more helpful than Rocío's people skills in this case.

Hala took control without missing a step. "But is such a machine possible? I know there have been experiments with compressed air and even ammonia." Hala made a dubious face. "Of course ammonia is poisonous, so I'm not sure that's advisable. We want your expert opinion on whether it's possible to create such a machine."

Hala paused expectantly but the inventor didn't seem ready to take the bait of flattery. When he didn't say anything, she added, "In fact we were thinking of investing in your washing machine venture."

Good idea, Hala.

"Invest, really?" He stepped forward involuntarily.

"The time savings and financial savings of your washing machine could be impressive, but a device that could keep items cool even in the hottest summer—that could revolutionize the way we eat—everything! Food production, trade, even medicine. But as I said, I'm not sure it's possible."

Rocío wasn't sure if it was the genuine enthusiasm in Hala's voice or the poke at his ego but he finally burst out with "But it is! It—" and then immediately clapped first one hand then the other over his mouth, dropping the gloves again.

"You can tell us," Hala coaxed.

"I can't." He shook his head.

"Did you sign a contract? A non-disclosure agreement?"

"Well, no," he said through his hands.

"So?"

"A handshake agreement."

"We're not competitors. Or investors. Yet," Hala said.

Oh, nice technique. "Anything you tell us won't harm your business, unless something illegal is going on, and you seem like the kind of man who wouldn't want to be involved in anything illegal," Rocío coaxed. "We need this information because someone has been hurt, and we want to stop other people from getting hurt. That's our job."

"A handshake agreement doesn't have the same legal standing as a signed contract." Hala touched one finger to the handle of a screwdriver, seeming not to watch him while still observing him intently. "It doesn't carry the same expectation of confidentiality."

He lowered his hands to his chest and moistened his lips. "I wouldn't want to be involved in anything illegal."

"You wouldn't," Hala agreed. "I can tell you're a good person. But you invented such a machine and now something seems wrong to you?"

"My investor—we came up with a working prototype."He didn't seem to notice he'd gone from denying any knowledge of such a machine to admitting he'd made one.

So, it is possible. This changes everything. Not a new infestation of MMFs? Not a new perpetrator at all? How long can this machine keep something cold? Since November? Rocío kept her questions behind her teeth, trusting Hala to get there and not wanting to break her growing rapport with Señorx Azimi.

"He said he wanted to show it to some colleagues, raise more interest and, and money."

"And?" Hala prodded gently.

"And I haven't seen him in three months. I can't find him." He rubbed his face. "All that work! And he took the plans! I've been trying to recreate them but I can't remember exactly which—"

"Since November?" Hala asked. "Would your machine keep something completely frozen all that time?"

He nodded repeatedly. "Of course, yes, my design *is* functional! I calculate that for six months only daily recharging would be needed, like a battery for a lamp, well, a little more powerful than a lamp. After that he would need the—well, it's proprietary, but it would need to be topped off. I thought if nothing else he would have to come back in six months. He would, right?"

"But you tried to find him?" Hala asked.

"Oh, yes, I went to the address he gave me." He squatted to gather up the gloves, then stood, chin tucked, kneading them in his hands. "It doesn't—there's nothing there and no one had heard of him. Or at the office he said he worked at."

"What name did he give you?"

"Ariano Hidalgo Ortega."

Rocío's heart thumped hard with excitement. Hidalgo Ortega. That name sounded familiar. What's more, she had heard...no, *read* it recently. Hidalgo y Ortega Cemetery. The image of the funerary card on Pilar's boat, tucked below the photo of Pilar's mother rose in her mind.

Hidalgo and Ortega were not that common as surnames, though they weren't unheard of. Pilar, this inventor and the cemetery could be connected. And what's more, there was a shelter there, the Eloisa de Hidalgo y Ortega Shelter for Indigents. Pilar's daughter's name was Eloisa. That couldn't be a coincidence. The search for Pilar had focused on the neighborhoods closest to the docks, which would be familiar territory for her. The cemetery and shelter were in the extreme northeast part of the city, but not far from where they were now. That was too many coincidences.

"Was there ever a woman with him?" Rocío asked, interrupting his vague description of the man—brown hair, brown eyes, young.

"No, he always came alone."

"Did he have an accent? Or, are you sure it was a man? Not a woman posing as a man?" She gestured down at her own masculine attire.

"No." He shook his head. "No, not a woman. Even I would notice that. And no accent. I mean," he frowned trying to recall, "he had a Benerex accent."

A Benerex man, with a cold machine, and a possible connection to Pilar, and a shelter where no one had searched for her. "Hala, did you get the specifics of the machine? Yes? Then we have to go."

CHAPTER 13

THE ELOISA DE HIDALGO y Ortega Shelter for Indigents was a cheery, sprawling sandstone building with thick oleander bushes growing against its walls. The blooms glowed pink and white in the bright sun. From where Rocío and Hala sat despondently on the low buff wall bounding a kitchen garden, they could see an open space where shrilly shouting kids played pelota-ya and the main entrances to the building and the grounds. Not that it helped, now.

"I can't believe we just missed her." Rocío groaned. "If only I'd thought of that perdido funerary card more quickly."

"Do you know how much stimulus the brain screens out as unimportant? Scientists posit at least ninety percent or we would be overwhelmed by everything entering our senses." Hala cleaned her spectacles with a soft piece of cloth, held them up the light and stowed them away again. "Of course without a direct way to observe the process, it's only theory, so you could just go on torturing yourself. That's a very useful way of figuring out what to do next."

Rocío huffed out a laugh and pressed her glass of water—provided by a kind man in the kitchen—against her temple, though it held only the memory of coolness. "Okay. Point taken. I'll stop wallowing. There must be some way to pick up Pilar's trail from here."

"We talked to everyone," Hala said, "and I'm not going back in there."

The scarily efficient woman in charge had been aghast that a criminal might be using her shelter for purposes not intended and had made sure that Rocío and Hala spoke to every person working, sheltering or visiting there, from the ninety-year old ex-cook sleeping in a rocker, to the smallest children in the brightly painted and not-too-shabby playroom. Pilar and her children had been here and gone again, unexceptional and almost unremarked, all indications of her river folk identity erased except for a slight accent the administrator hadn't been able to place.

"There are two other shelters in La Bene." Hala raked her hands through her hair, leaving it sticking out in all directions. "Which would she have gone to?"

"On opposite sides of the city. If we guess wrong we'll miss her again. What is she doing?" Rocío switched the glass to her other temple and brooded. "Are you...I'm becoming uncomfortable with the idea of Pilar as our suspect." She gestured broadly at the shelter. "This is the kind of place you come to when you have nothing left. She has a family, a boat, employment. What would make her give all that up?"

"People don't think things through." Hala shifted her position on the wall. "It's hard to reconcile, however, with the amount of planning needed to use the MMF. This plan, or the seed of it, probably started in November. That's the only time she could have gotten an MMF—"

"We hope."

"—and that's the same time the cold machine was stolen. By a man."

"Hala." Rocío almost dropped her glass in her excitement. "Was Pilar even here in November? How long did she say it takes to travel between here and Kooja Ya? That's the only time she could have gotten an MMF, right? If we know that we'll know if she's our suspect. Probably."

Hala closed her eyes and tipped her head back, either to recall what Pilar had said or to do the math herself. "An average of twenty-one days upriver and eighteen down." She opened her eyes. "No, that's no help without actual records. It's likely she was here in early to mid November."

Rocío slouched again, though she wasn't sure why she was disappointed. They didn't have another suspect, unless they counted the unidentified man who had stolen the cold machine.

The gate creaked open. Rocío shaded her eyes to get a better look, just in case it was Pilar. No, the shape and especially the hair was wrong. This woman had painfully short hair. Silvia? What was she doing here? Rocío nudged Hala with her elbow.

"She is unexpected, isn't she? Never where you planned." Hala jumped down from the wall and headed off to intercept her.

Rocío trailed a few steps behind to observe Silvia's body language.

Silvia waved with her whole arm when she spotted Hala and angled around the ball field to meet them. *That was unambiguous.*

"Silvia, what are you doing here?" Hala asked.

"Detectives, what are you doing here?" Silvia asked, overlapping with Hala. "Sorry."

"You first," Hala said.

Silvia leaned towards Hala. "I've been chasing complaints against *The Resolute* all over the city." She rummaged in her leather satchel and took out a notebook, flipping to a page near the back.

"Let's go stand in the shade," Rocío said and led them under the outstretched branches of a dark gomero tree.

"I noticed the complaints in the harbormaster's ledgers the other day and I went back and asked if it was normal to have so many against one boat. Suspected contraband, noise violations, tax evasion, smuggling, incorrect signal flags, illegal disposal of sewage, failure to pay water fees. The harbormaster said no. So I looked at the complainants: Sujay Suárez Gomis—Sujay is Pilar's cousin's name, the one that went to the Hospital, and unusual enough that it made me wonder if it was a fake—Costas Páez Biel—Costas, of course, we all know, the captain—Buenaventura—the second mate's name—Páez Ferreira, Arjan Biel Serafini, Finn Azimi Ferrar—"

Hala made a soft noise at the inventor's name.

"—and Stéfano Hidalgo Ortega. I traced them across the city and I found more complaints against Pilar. Child abuse in Sanblas district, a restraining order in Palmeira, a contest of custody by a city official in Arabasca—those last two are obviously neighborhoods near the docks so it's plausible someone would make a complaint against Pilar there, but I couldn't find the any real people behind the complainants' names. It looks like someone has a serious vendetta against Pilar, going back to October of last year."

"Do they?" Rocío said softly. They had just said Pilar seemed like an unlikely suspect. Was she being framed in an escalating feud? Or had she finally taken revenge against its instigator? Her brother, the captain of the boat? Or someone else?

"And Hidalgo Ortega brought you here?" Hala asked.

"Yes, I didn't know the other surnames, but this seemed the obvious—"

"Wait." Rocío held up a forestalling hand and Silvia stopped immediately, looking apprehensive.

"I do. We just met Finn Azimi Ferrar. And Costas was married to a, wait..." Rocío bit her lip. "Ruben Biel Páez, and Pilar to an Ariano Serafini Verdugo. And Ferreira is a different form of Ferrar. Someone mixed and matched surnames to come up with aliases."

Silvia let out a relieved breath. "To point the finger away from themselves?"

"Or subconsciously point the finger at themselves," Hala said. "It happens more often than you'd think. A way of boasting about what they've done. Did you get a description of the person or persons who made the complaints?"

Silvia flipped through her notebook again, more to give herself something to do than because she needed it, Rocío thought. "It's not useful, other than that it's a man, so if it's Pilar trying to undermine her brother, she has a partner. Youngish, average height, average looking, like most Benerex of Iberex descent, nice brown hair, brown eyes, low bridged nose and flat profile. No distinguishing anything."

The inventor's description had been vaguer but still consistent. And it described the inventor himself, though maybe not "young." But as Silvia said, it also described half the men in La Bene. "No spectacles?" Rocío asked, just in case it was the inventor pursuing revenge for Pilar stealing the cold machine. Though no one would describe his hair as "nice."

"No spectacles." Silvia looked around at the bucolic scene as one of the children yelled in particular excitement. "But what are you doing here?"

"Among her things, Pilar had a funerary card for the Eloisa de Hidalgo y Ortega Cemetery. And she was here." Rocío hit her thigh in exasperation. "But we missed her."

"Did you try the cemetery?" Silvia asked.

"There's a small graveyard in the back, but there's just a few headstones, and nowhere to hide," Hala said.

"No, I mean the Eloisa de Hidalgo y Ortega Cemetery."

Hala looked at her blankly. "Isn't that the graveyard?"

Silvia pursed her lips. "No, the big one. I mean comparatively. It's not that big."

"I don't know what you mean." Hala looked a question at Rocío, who shrugged. She didn't either.

"The Violetta Consolação Memorial Cemetery. It used to be the Eloisa de Hidalgo y Ortega Cemetery. It was renamed."

Hala looked pained. "How did I not know that? When was this?"

"Um. At least six years ago? I only know because I have family buried there. And everyone always called it the Violetta Consolação anyway, because she's buried there, so you probably wouldn't know unless you had old funerary cards like I do."

"We were on Isla de los lobos then," Hala murmured.

Rocío squelched the memory that wanted to rise up at the reminder. "And our families both use the Eastern Cemetery. There's no reason we would know."

"I should have known."

"Yes, let's stand here in recrimination." Rocío poked Hala in the side.

Hala swatted Rocío's hand away. "If you'd let me finish, I was saying I should have known because the Violetta Consolação Cemetery is the perfect place to hide because of all the people living there."

CHAPTER 14

"This is a disgrace." Rocío's lips twisted in disgust as she looked around the graveyard-turned-slum, not for the people forced to make the best of a bad situation, but for government inefficiency that had abandoned them.

Small children played pelota-ya on the flat tops of chest tombs, their shouts as joyful as those of the children at the shelter, but their movements constricted by lack of space. Along the back edge of the cemetery, adults sat in the entrances of tilted mausoleums built of the same warm sandstone as the shelter. The last light of the day glowed gold on the fancy monuments to the dead and on the living, their hard hands busy with laundry in buckets, sorting sugared peanuts into twists of paper or other small jobs to bring in centavo by centavo something to live on, with the smallest children at their feet. Clothes lines flapped with graying laundry, obscuring and revealing older children lugging buckets of water or scrap wood to fuel the cooking fires. A fug of cooking beans, tortillas stretched with some bitter, cheaper flour, and human waste hung over the graveyard. It stung Rocío's eyes and the inside of her nose. Chickens scratched under spindly monkey puzzle trees in one corner, the ground bare soil. A goat bleated.

Two years ago, Hala had told them, a sinkhole had opened up in Marietta district, swallowing two tenements and cracking the foundations and walls of dozens more. The district council had evicted the tenants for their safety but had failed to give them anywhere to move to. The ones with nowhere else to go had ended up here, in limbo.

Rocío remembered hearing about the sinkhole, but a family drama had engulfed her and she'd missed the aftermath.

"They've petitioned the House of Refugees every month since, but with no effect." Hala scanned the rows of tombs as she talked. "There," she said in a low voice, indicating a far corner.

Pilar sat on a scrap of cloth, her children leaning on her, their faces smudged with dirt and exhaustion. All traces of their river folk heritage that could be removed had been: the distinctive trousers, vest and heavy gold earrings were replaced with an unexceptional huiple, kilt and a Benerex hairdo. She was one of the few people with nothing in her hands to keep her busy, her very stillness making her stand out.

Silvia hesitated, her eyes flicking anxiously over all the people between her and Pilar, and seemed to withdraw into herself. Sudden worry tightened Rocío's back; she'd seen that reaction from people who had been abused, their flight or fight reaction on a hair trigger. She couldn't let Silvia go in there.

Hala had already stepped into the cemetery, heading straight to Pilar, masked by two older men talking animatedly.

"Silvia," Rocío said quietly, "can you go get more advocates from the CJC?"

Silvia's face froze. "I don't need special treatment."

"That's not what—"

"I know what you meant. I pull my own weight." Silvia stomped off on a path diagonal to Hala's, and Rocío followed, trying to keep an eye on everyone at once. Silvia swung around to the side, picking a path between the graves, a child on a tricycle and a teenager picking stones out of beans. He shook back his shaggy hair and watched them with flat, suspicious eyes.

Pilar looked up as they closed in, her face blank. She rose with terrible slowness, her body stiff, braced for a blow she'd been waiting for. Her son glared at them, alive to his mother's fear, while the girl hid her face in his back.

"My brother?" Pilar asked through stiff lips.

"He still lives." Rocío's tone made it clear this was not the good fortune it sounded.

They were attracting more attention. The teenager set his beans aside, his big hands open on his knees, and an old man leaned on his cane and watched them with cynical eyes.

"You need to come with us," Hala said.

Pilar's laugh cracked out of her, harsh and short. A few more people stopped to watch.

"Pilar, are these people bothering you?" A pregnant woman dried her soapy hands on her shirt and walked nearer.

"They have the *right*," Pilar said bitterly. Her daughter whimpered. Pilar softened her voice, but the edge was still there, and something shifted in her eyes, from blankness to the ferocity of a cornered dog that would snap and bite to escape. "They're *advocates*."

"And what do they think you've done?" The old man tapped his cane against a tombstone. There was no give in his voice. A few more people drifted closer.

With a chill, Rocío realized she had misjudged the situation. She had thought these people were too focused on their own survival to care about Pilar, but obviously they were a tight community and Pilar had been accepted in. Rocío had also thought they would hold the same prejudice against river folk that others in La Bene had shown and that they wouldn't care about advocates removing one from their midst. That had obviously been a mistake. Whether they knew Pilar better than expected or were angry at city authorities, they did care and weren't interested in making this easy. Rocío, Hala and Silvia shouldn't have come in here alone. There were too many people around them who were too vulnerable and too close to the edge already.

And too close to a mob, with no clear path of exit, between the tree roots, the broken but cared for tombs, the tricycle, the pregnant woman, the children. Plus an inexperienced advocate already on the edge. Tension crept up Rocío's lower back to her shoulders, arms and hands.

She met Hala's glance and saw the same awareness there. Hala leaned against a headstone, seemingly relaxed, in a pose that gave her a view of the people behind them.

"Pilar," Rocío began some conciliatory phrase, but Pilar spoke over her.

"Killed my brother to inherit his boat."

"What are you doing living here, then?" the old man asked.

"I'm a poor murderer," Pilar said. Her lips drew off her teeth in a snarl.

"We could have told them that." The pregnant woman stepped in front of Pilar's children, blocking them from view, one hand supporting the weight of her stomach. "You're not wanted here."

"We came to listen," Rocío said in her most soothing voice, spreading her hands in invitation. She hoped Silvia would stay quiet and not break the tension into rash and dangerous action.

"Sure you did," the teenager sneered. "People always come here to listen—not fine us or threaten us or blame us for having nowhere else to live."

An ugly murmur ran through the crowd. "You should go," the old man said, snapping his cane against stone. Thwack. *Thwack.*

Silvia flinched away from the sound, her eyes flaring wide with fear and unseeing. For a moment she froze, and then another reaction swept in. Her head reared back and her jaw tensed.

"Silvia, no," Rocío said, recognizing the signs of a person reacting to being pushed past the limit, all her boundaries violated by the person who had hurt her, her bodily integrity breached, the things she believed about herself undermined, making her afraid again, when she thought the fear had ended. Making her lash out to reassert control, no matter that the person who had hurt her wasn't here.

Rocío reached for her helplessly, knowing that touching her was the last thing she should do.

"That's not going to happen," Silvia grated out, reaching for her baton.

"I didn't do anything," Pilar shouted, her voice shaking.

A rock sailed out of the crowd and cracked into Silvia's shoulder. She flicked open her baton.

Rocío smacked her hand down.

Silvia glared at her, unseeing, her eyes narrowed to slits. She turned on Rocío, half raising her baton again.

"Silvia. Stop." Rocío's voice shook with the effort to keep it calm. "I am not your enemy. These people are not your enemy."

Putting the lie to her words, another rock shot out of the crowd, narrowly missing both of them. Someone else cried out in pain.

Hala was talking to the old man, trying to reason a way out for all of them. Rocío barely heard her. She held Silvia's unseeing stare with her own and summoned every ounce of persuasion in her body. "Silvia, you have to stay in control. They're not here, whoever hurt you is not here. These people aren't the ones who hurt you." *Though they might.* The people around them were menacing shapes in her side vision. She thought Hala had persuaded the old man to step back, but she wasn't sure. "*You're better than this.*"

Silvia blinked rapidly. A sob shuddered through her, shaking the baton in her hand.

Rocío raised her open hands as she stepped forward, projecting *I'm not going to hurt you or push you.* The younger woman stepped back, her eyes opening wider, awareness coming back into them. Her face flushed with shame, and her pupils flared. She lowered the baton.

"Steady." Rocío kept her eyes linked with Silvia's.

Hala plucked Rocío's sleeve, tugging her towards the exit. Rocío followed, trying to watch behind her and the path and Silvia. Silvia trembled but stuck close, her baton clasped along her leg now. The inhabitants pressed in without touching, barely shifting out of the way, muttering angrily, an occasional word tossed up. "Perdidos bullies!" The air seemed too thick and hard to breathe.

They reached the edge of the cemetery.

The crowd followed them to the gates but no further, their presence pushing against Rocío like magnets repelling, demanding they leave. The teenager and the pregnant woman bulked in the opening, watching them like a warning, and the sounds of upset people roiled behind them. "Don't come back!" an anonymous voice shouted. "Ancestors forget you!"

Rocío sucked in a breath at this respite, automatically scanning the quiet, tree-lined street for threats and bystanders that might get embroiled in their mess. The evening outside their bubble of animosity was quiet. Crickets chirped. A horse and carriage clopped down the street, the driver humming.

Only a few people strolled by in the twilight, looking curiously in their direction, but not stopping. Two school kids in sarongs with satchels bulging with books, a few workers, a family with three children. The streetlights turned on, catching in their warm glow a person watching them. Rocío's eyes locked on that familiar-unfamiliar figure. She couldn't place him for a moment—an average looking young man.

Tears leaked down Silvia's cheeks and her shoulders hunched. "I'm sorry."

"Wait, Silvia, not yet," she said quickly, sympathetically. In a lower voice, she asked herself, "Who is that? I know him..." Tension, momentarily lulled by the peace of street and the symbolic barrier between them and the people in the cemetery, moved up her arms and down her back like a cramp.

"What?" Silvia asked thickly, snorting back her tears. She followed Rocío's gaze.

The question unlocked the answer. "The nurse from the Hospital. What is he doing here?"

CHAPTER 15

As if Rocío's question were a signal, the nurse jogged over, relief lightening his eyes. He didn't seem to notice the semi-mob at their backs. "It's you! Did you find her?"

He smiled hesitantly, and Rocío found herself smiling back in response to his warmth. Without the little nursing cap, her initial impression that he had beautiful hair was reconfirmed, glossy and perfectly coiffed with slightly expensive pins holding the loops and knots in place.

"What do you mean?" Hala stepped in front of him, bringing him to a halt. "What are you doing here?"

"Walking home. But then I saw you, and I thought you might not know…"

The whispers behind them gained force. Uneasiness coiled through Rocío. "Maybe we could move away?" the people in the cemetery were too close to violence, and the word *MMFs* or an accusation against Pilar might push them over the edge into real violence.

"I want to hear what he has to say!" the pregnant woman called.

Why? Rocío didn't like this. Silvia was a wary presence at her side, the tears wiped away, a thin veneer of professionalism restored, at least outwardly. Hala's back was pulled up straight with tension, ratcheting Rocío's higher.

"Please start from the beginning. What is your interest in us and what are you doing here?" Hala asked.

He seemed taken aback by her detached tone and offered his tentative smile again, revealing one appealingly crooked front tooth.

Again Rocío wanted to smile back, but this time the impulse made her suspicious. Why was he exuding so much charm? It dripped off him like honey, trying to ensnare...what?

"I'm the nurse from the Hospital. I was there when you came in?" he said confidingly. "About...you know?"

"We know," Rocío said.

"I was walking home, and I saw you. And you haven't been to the Hospital, so I thought maybe you didn't know..."

"Know what?" Hala asked.

He dipped his head. "That Costas—the man you brought in—he didn't make it. He died a few hours ago." He peeked at them from beneath his lashes. "I'm sorry."

Rocío barely tasted her own bitter failure and shock before Pilar shrieked and hurtled out of the gates. "Liar!"

Rocío caught her by one arm, pulling the woman close, half hug, half restraint. Pilar fought, flailing, still screaming, her nails raking across Rocío's forearm, her head smacking into Rocío's chin. Rocío's vision went bright with pain and Pilar pulled them off balance in her single minded rush forward. Rocío staggered. Silvia captured Pilar's other arm, a counterweight, and steadied them both.

For another moment Pilar struggled wildly, harsh grunts of pain escaping her. Rocío's own throat ached with the memory of what that pain felt like. And then Pilar dropped, limp, like all her muscles had betrayed her, her weight almost pulling Rocío down with her. Sobs tore through her body.

"Liar," Pilar wailed more softly. "Liar."

Rocío braced her, held her up against the sobs that tried to tear her down.

The nurse's face was still pleasant and concerned when Rocío looked up. She wondered what she would have seen if she'd been watching him the whole time, and she didn't know why he disturbed her, besides the charm. She followed Hala's frowning gaze to Pilar's children.

They clung to each other just inside the gates, frozen and afraid to move, like a rabbit under the eye of a hawk, with memories of blood and anger smeared across their faces. They looked shrunken, as if they were trying to disappear, the tendons in their little necks straining as they tried to anticipate what would happen next, their gazes pinned to the nurse. Rocío's hands tightened involuntarily on Pilar and the other woman moaned, but didn't struggle.

Rocío recognized that body language. Victims of abuse looked like that in the presence of their abuser. Especially children. Her gaze swung back to the nurse.

"Look at the way they're standing," Silvia breathed.

"I remember," Rocío said. He'd said *I just came on shift* and, holding a stuffed bunny, *I was just returning this. One of the children must have dropped it.* Those two statements didn't go together. How had he known one of Pilar's children had dropped a toy if he hadn't seen them come in? And then Pilar's crewmates had exploded into desperate action, just like Pilar had now. Not at the sight of more advocates as Rocío had thought, but at the sight of this nurse? At the threat the toy represented?

The pieces rearranged themselves in her head with a click, showing a very different picture. Not Pilar manipulating events, but him?

Pilar lifted her head, choking her sobs down.

Hala, responding to something she heard in Rocío's voice, shifted again, positioning herself for a takedown.

"What's your name?" Rocío asked.

"Ariano."

"Ariano?" Silvia asked.

"Ariano Serafini Verdugo," Rocío said flatly. She shifted Pilar into Silvia's grip. "Pilar's ex-spouse."

"Arjan Biel Serafini," Silvia whispered. "That was one of the names on the complaints. Arjan is another way of saying Ariano. Serafini is not a common surname. It was you. You made all those complaints."

Hala's breath hissed through her teeth.

"What?" He drew himself up. "I don't know what you mean. I saw you—I was trying to *help*. Whatever is happening is *dangerous*."

He was good. So good. Maybe he even believed what he was saying. The best liars did.

Rocío wanted to believe him. She would have, if they were alone. If she didn't have the evidence of the children's behavior. And the discrepancy in what he'd said before. He had an incredible amount of charisma—as a diplomat he could have ended wars and as a politician he could have started them. Instead he hit his children and his spouse and hid his crimes with more acts of cruelty.

"I saw your marriage contract," Rocío said. "Pilar was married to you."

"Me?" He pressed both hands to his chest in surprised supplication. "Ask her."

Even no longer touching her, Rocío felt the shudder move through Pilar. The other woman's gaze fastened on the metal tupu, where Ariano's thumbs and fingers overlapped it.

People were always getting stabbed by tupus, either accidentally or in fights. The ornamental pins had to be sharp to pierce through wool serapes, and most were large. His was ten centimeters, as long as Rocío's palm was wide. The pin itself was as thick as an awl. The holes they left in people's skin were small, jagged and painful. Easy to inflict. Easy to hide. Abusers were good at hiding evidence of their violence.

In spite of his smiling face, Rocío didn't have any doubt that this was Pilar's ex-spouse, and that he beat her and his children. Body language didn't lie. She didn't doubt that he had harassed them through La Bene with false complaints. It was a common abuser's tactic, as if they all had the same playbook, an instinctive knowledge of how to hurt and control, a dark mirror to Rocío's understanding of human nature. But what did that have to do with MMFs? She still didn't have all the pieces.

"Pilar, is he lying? Were you married?" Silvia asked gently.

Pilar seemed unable to speak, caught in a staring contest with Ariano.

"Pilar?" Silvia asked, strain threading through her voice. She shifted Pilar's stiff weight to Rocío. Ariano's eyelids dipped, shielding his eyes. Pilar shuddered again.

"You can trust me," Silvia said quietly. "I'll *believe* you." She pushed up her long sleeve, revealing five mottled purple and yellow bruises ringing her arm, evenly spaced ovals like fingers, like someone's fist had grabbed on and *squeezed*. "You can tell *me*, Pilar."

Pilar's neck creaked as she turned her head away from Ariano, first to look down at the bruises, then up to Silvia's face, and back again to Ariano. Unease flickered in his eyes.

"Yes," she whispered.

"Tell me," Silvia urged.

"Yes!" The word burst out of Pilar and she threw back her head in defiance, pulling free of Rocío's hands.

"He's lying! He killed Costas and I ran because he'll kill me next and take my children because he can't *stand* the thought of them being raised as river folk. He can't *stand* that I left him. He thought I would stay forever and let him beat me and my children. He said no one would believe me.

"He said because I was a foreigner, *river folk*, everyone would believe him. And even if they believed me they wouldn't care. That I deserved it, because I'm river folk. That we deserved it," she said more softly, not looking at her children. She trembled so hard her teeth chattered together.

Silvia hooked a hand under Pilar's arm, her own breath coming fast in dismay.

Shock coursed over Ariano's face. He hadn't thought Pilar would speak. Almost immediately it morphed into an expression of benevolent concern. Rocío would have missed it if she hadn't been watching so closely. Unobtrusively, Hala shifted closer to him.

"Me?" Ariano said, his fingers fluttering against his chest. "I would never do that. I'm a nurse. I help people. I was just trying to help. There's something wrong with her."

"That's what they always say," Silvia said.

Pilar's breath shuddered through her.

The people in the cemetery, almost forgotten until now, muttered behind them. Rocío turned to see Pilar's children sheltered behind the protective bulk of the pregnant woman.

"I *know*," Silvia said, addressing them. She held her arm up so they could see, flinching but determined.

A whisper ran through the watching crowd. The pressure building up had a different feel this time. Rocío could almost taste it, like metal on her tongue, a magnetic force reversing itself, so that the opposite ends of the magnets aligned. The pregnant woman's eyes narrowed, in speculation this time, not anger.

"You don't believe *her*?" Ariano said, his innocent facade cracking again, exposing a sliver of indignation.

Hala cocked her head at Rocío, the question clear as if she had spoken it: *What do you want to do?*

Am I reading them right? She's been wrong just moments before about the crowd and how they'd react. She ran her gaze over them, the pregnant woman protectively shielding Pilar's children, the teenager with his hands clenching and unclenching, not looking at the advocates any more but the nurse. Had he sipped powerlessness, living among the dead, and would he focus on the authority of the city, in the bodies of the advocates, or on one man hurting one woman and her children? Specific and right in front of him, not a distant, faceless target. The old man with the cane, his arthritic fingers as tight around it as they could bend, his shoulders rounded with age, but not his spirit, if those glaring eyes were any indication.

She measured them all, drew on her knowledge of people, learned in the vigilance in her parents' home and then on her own as an actor and as an advocate, evaluated all the little signs of body language, pinched lips and torsos leaning forward and mostly the feet, pointing at Pilar and the nurse.

Rocío turned to Hala and made a throwing away gesture, giddy at the turns of tension and at staking such an important investigation on feet.

Not just feet. Years of experience and a good partner to back her up.

Hala smiled fleetingly at Rocío before turning to Pilar. "What about the dead MMF? Where did it come from?"

A growl came from the cemetery people. A smile flickered over Ariano's lips, there and gone, as he judged the other way from Rocío. They would see, who was right and who was wrong.

"He put it on my boat. He had to have." Pilar stared defiantly at Ariano, still shaking. "It wasn't me. We met—we met that sick foreigner who created them—but years before! I didn't know. I didn't know!"

"Me?" Ariano fell back a step, his gesture at the tupu more overt this time.

Pilar's lips peeled back from her teeth, but that was not a smile.

"But why an MMF?" Hala pursued her question. "Why not kill you? Why your brother?"

"Because he wants to hurt me and he still thought he could get me back—"

"This is nonsense!"

"—and he *hates* seeing his children as foreigners. Isn't that right, Ariano?" Pilar's voice had dropped almost to a whisper, but it gained force again. "I know how you think. I had to, to survive, to protect my children. They even speak Benerex with an accent now." She slid a glance at Rocío. "Maybe that's what pushed him over the edge when he saw them in November. He wants them, body and soul, he wants them to hate me and everything about my heritage." Pilar's voice steadied, fierce with the savage pleasure of someone who'd had to swallow it all down, take it and suffer, finally free to drag it all out into the light and point it like a weapon at the person who had hurt her children. "What better way than to make it look like the river folk had brought the plague back to La Bene? My children would believe everything their father said about their evil mother. They would hate me and he would win."

Rocío's fingers curled into her palms. Pilar's explanation for the MMFs made more sense than any of the muddled theories involving her as the culprit. An abuser would do anything he thought he could get away with to keep control and paint his victim as the monster in his place.

He had risked panicking an entire city in his monomania, had dredged up one of Rocío's worst fears, dragged it back onto center stage with his grandiose, pathetic scheme. Because he was so little he measured himself by how small he could make others. How dare he? How dare he use the threat of MMFs against La Bene? *Against me?* Rocío's professional detachment started to slip, anger flushing her face and ears hot, sitting like a burning coal in her chest. Her vision went tight and dark on Ariano. She willed Pilar to keep pushing. Rocío could arrest him for assault on Pilar's word, but she wanted more, she wanted to arrest him for the MMFs.

"This is nonsense!" Ariano crossed his arms and shook his head at them like a benevolent patriarch. "I have no idea what this woman is talking about."

A sob shuddered through Pilar again but she held his eyes.

His lips tightened.

"You've gone too far this time, Ariano," Pilar said, her voice flat and strained thin. Her pulse beat too rapidly in her neck. "They have to find out the truth about the MMFs. It's too big. You made a *mistake.*" She leaned hard on the last word, like a virtuoso on their chosen instrument and finally got an unstudied reaction from him.

Ariano stalked forward, hands clenching into fists, the benign facade slipping and revealing the rage beneath. "*I did not!*"

Pilar stood her ground, shaking.

Rocío stepped forward protectively in spite of herself. Hala mirrored her, closing in.

He checked himself though, lowered his voice and regained control. He flashed a pained smile at Rocío and Hala. "I don't know what she means."

"It seems that you do," Rocío said dryly.

He sucked in a harsh breath, fear finally touching his face. He swung back to Pilar. "Tell them you're the one who made a mistake," he said through his teeth.

Pilar flinched. "No."

"Tell them," he growled, his hands twitching.

"No!"

"Mami!" Pilar's little girl sobbed, great heaving cries with words caught inside. "Daddy, don't hurt mami."

"You stupid brat, I told you to shut up." He jerked forward, hand raising for a slap.

Pilar lurched into his way, panic shaking her fixed expression away, too fast for Hala to interfere.

Ariano shoved Pilar with both of his hands on her shoulders. She fell backwards, catching herself on her hands, into Rocío's approach.

At the same time, Silvia lunged forward wildly, blocking Hala. "No!"

Pilar swung her feet around and tripped Ariano. Silvia danced out of the way, glee lighting up her face.

Screeching, he fell into the street and skidded on his hands. "You stupid shit puddle excuse for—" He scrabbled to get up.

Hala pushed him down with her foot on his back. "Stop!"

He struggled against her. "You can't do this to me. I'm an upstanding citizen, you can't believe her, she's no one."

"Señorx, please stop moving, or I will be forced to use stronger measures," Hala said, the muscles standing out in her jaw.

"Look at her! You can't believe her over me. I'm from here. I have a good job. She's no one, rabble, a dirty foreigner. You can't do this to me!"

The old man from the cemetery hobbled over surprisingly quickly and pressed the tip of his cane into Ariano's back next to Hala's foot. "Hurry up and arrest him, or I'm going to do it myself. A citizen's arrest."

"Wait," Rocío called. "Silvia, you should do it." She helped Pilar sit up while her children swarmed over her, hugging every body part they could reach.

"Me? Are you sure?" Silvia stared at her, open mouthed.

"Yes, you." Rocío grinned at her, the muscles loosening in her back and her anger sliding away into relief.

"Right." Silvia straightened her shoulders, her eyes lighting with fierce anticipation. She knelt next to Ariano and secured his hands with restraints, not roughly but thoroughly. "Señorx, if you could remove your cane and step back?"

Hala and Silvia lifted Ariano to his feet. His face was twisted and purple with ugly rage, the pleasant facade cracked wide open. "You're going to pay for this. You'll see. This is all your fault." Locks of hair fell out of his pins and caught on the blood beading on his cheek.

Rocío would bet this was the spouse and father Pilar and his children knew most often, though the blood spilled had been theirs and not his.

Pilar stiffened, raising her chin. She climbed to her feet and tucked her children into a protective hug, one on each side of her. "Would you please wait a moment." She bent and said something too softly to be overheard.

The kids raised their chins in imitation of their mother. "*Watch this,*" Pilar instructed them, her accent thicker than before. "Remember this when you get scared. He's not going to hurt us anymore. They're stopping him, right now."

"You don't know what you're doing, you—"

"Señorx Ariano Serafini Verdugo, you are under arrest for assault and battery against Pilar of *The Resolute* and her two children, also of *The Resolute*. Also for inciting mayhem and riot, at least one act of terrorism, and the murder of Costas of *The Resolute*."

Pilar's chin shook and she blinked back tears. The kids watched with wide eyes.

"You have the right to tell your story to an adjudicator and to be judged by a jury of your peers." He opened his mouth to spew more invective and Silvia cut him off with newfound firmness. "Every time you speak, I will add a count of public abuse and endangering the well-being of minors. Two actually, since there are two children present." She beamed at Rocío, who nodded in approval.

Ariano snapped his mouth closed. He didn't look repentant or even aware that he was wrong, but he did look thwarted. Meanwhile, Pilar looked at least five centimeters taller, and the kids' didn't look so much like they were pressed between two weights. Even Silvia didn't look so pinched in her extreme thinness. That was a good enough start for Rocío.

Now if she could just be sure the MMFs were not threatening her city. "Pilar," Rocío started and then stopped, not sure how to go on. Up until five minutes ago, Pilar had seen them as her enemy and probably still would not want to say anything that would get her in trouble now.

"You want to know what I know about the MMFs," Pilar said, her hands tightening and loosening on her kids' shoulders.

"I want to protect my city and the people in it, yes," Rocío said carefully. *Including your children.* She didn't say it, but she thought Pilar didn't need her to. "Do you know anything?"

Ariano glared and bristled threateningly. Pilar kept her eyes on Rocío.

"We could step away," Rocío said. "There's no reason he has to hear anything we say. It would help me, you and everyone in La Bene."

Pilar's lips tightened and she stepped out of his hearing distance. They both kept Ariano in sight.

"I don't know very much," she said in a low voice. "I know he's never been to Enkladt and I know he could never make MMFs himself. I don't think—What is she doing?"

Hala had put on her spectacles and crouched in front of Ariano. She stared intently at his feet, still clad, this hot evening, in sensible, rubber-soled shoes, meant for standing all day and protecting the wearer's feet from the hazards of the nursing profession: vomit, blood and other bodily fluids. Hala ran her hand her over hair, actually making it look a little tamer than usual."

Please lift your right foot." She looked up and added mildly, "If you attempt to kick me, I will add assaulting an advocate to the charges against you. It's also likely you will lose your balance and fall. We will intervene, but if we are not quick enough, as you are restrained, you won't be able to catch yourself with your hands. I assume you're familiar with the injuries that can occur as a result of... your work as nurse? They *are* painful. I know you're capable of restraint, or you wouldn't have manufactured a plan that required months of planning and waiting."

Ariano's eyes widened and then narrowed again as he absorbed Hala's double warning. "Are you threatening me?"

"I can see how it would be difficult for you to understand the difference between a threat and a statement of consequences. I'm stating a consequence."

Rocío motioned Pilar to stay back and moved closer to Ariano, ready to intervene if necessary. *It will be.*

He lifted his foot.

Hala dropped her eyes to his torso. If he tried to kick her, the movement would originate there and she could dodge. She untied his right shoe, slipped it off and turned it over. "Hmm." She pried at the inner edge of the sole and suddenly she had two pieces in her hand. She shook one and a something fell out, ringing metallically against the cobblestones. A key.

"Much simpler than a Jeen puzzle box." Hala smiled to herself. An answering smile lifted Rocío's lips. Hala picked up the key, turning it over in her long fingers. "What have we here?"

"How did you know?" Silvia asked.

"I could see that the sole of his right shoe was thicker than the left, although—"

"Hala," Rocío warned her as Ariano shifted his weight. She grabbed his arms and yanked back. At the same time, Hala pushed out of the way and Ariano kicked, missing her by half a meter. "That's another charge against you. Attempted assault on an advocate," Rocío said. He tried to pull away from her and she held him in place easily. "A taste of your own medicine too much for you?"

"Not so capable of restraint, now, are you? It must be important." Hala smirked at him.

Seres celestiales, she's feeling proud of herself. She stayed there on purpose.

Ariano went still, even his breath stopping.

"Can you tell what it's for?" Rocío asked Hala.

"You don't have to guess," Pilar said. "I know."

CHAPTER 16

"THAT'S IT! That's my cold machine!" The inventor jabbed his finger at a rectangular metal box.

The three of them—Rocío, Hala and Finn Azimi—stood in the open doorway to Ariano Serafini's secret one-room apartment. It was in a building at the extreme southern edge of La Bene, right where Pilar had told them it would be. One night while Pilar was still married to Ariano, she had followed him, hoping for proof that he had broken the monogamy clause and therefore their marriage contract.

Rocío and Hala had asked Finn to accompany them to identify his machine, if it was there, which would be used as evidence against Ariano and also, almost more importantly, lay to rest fears about the MMFs. Letting Rocío, and La Bene, go back to normal. Or at least what passed for normal now. The city, and Rocío, were never going to be able to return to what they were before plague and the threat of plague shaped their lives. Every time she realized that, she felt a pang of sadness through her entire body.

When Pilar gave them the address, Ariano had screamed and struggled, throwing himself at her, even with his hands restrained behind his back, his face an ugly mask of rage. Right now he should be in a holding room at the Sanblas CJC, while Silvia reported to her chief, and Pilar should be restored to her family on her boat, minus her brother Costas, who really had died during the day.

"Can I examine it? To see if it's damaged?" Finn asked.

"Let us check it first." Rocío stepped through the mess of folders, books and pamphlets stacked on the floor.

Unfortunately for Pilar, it was unlikely Ariano had been using this place for assignations, unless they were the paid kind. There was a narrow mattress in one corner, a tiny counter in another with a stack of metal dishes and mugs, easy to heat with magic with a sink and a hotplate with the magic battery exposed underneath, and an open cabinet stocked with basic foodstuffs. The rest of the apartment was crowded with tables with papers on them and under them, chairs loaded with boxes, and trays full of pens, markers, stencils, glue and paintbrushes. There was one window, with a cheap curtain pulled across it and paint cans lined up beneath it on the floor.

"Stay there," Hala told Finn.

"How does it open?" Rocío called to him. She ran her hands over the top, feeling a low vibration. "It seems to be on."

Hala found the catches on the sides and snapped them open.

"Wait, do you think—"

Hala lifted off the lid, revealing a white interior and the snarling little monster face of a malarial mosquito fairy.

"Ack!" Rocío shrieked and fell back a step.

"It's dead!" Hala said.

"What is it?" Finn shouted.

"I know that!" Rocío put a hand to her chest, feeling her heart pounding through skin and muscle and bone, and concentrated on breathing the fear back down into the place it seemed to permanently live now, under her sternum, always waiting to reach back up and grab her. The MMF was motionless, crumpled at the bottom of the box, its face twisted even in death.

"Then why are you shouting?" Finn asked.

"It scared me, okay? It's a little monster that killed a lot of people, almost including me and Hala. Seres celestiales, Hala, don't do that." Rocío rubbed her chest, her heart beat slowing.

"My apologies." Hala reached in with a gloved hand, ignoring

Rocío's undignified squeak, and picked up a little brown vial. She turned it to read the label. "*Petasum sulphuris*. That's a type of poisonous mushroom. Costas was dead as soon as Ariano gave him this," she said heavily.

"He really didn't expect to get caught."

"Can I examine my cold box now?" Finn called.

"Yes, although you understand it will have to be catalogued as evidence, don't you?"

"Yes, I just want to see if it's damaged."

"It's cold," Rocío said.

Hala handed Finn a pair of gloves. "Do not touch the MMF."

"No, of course not." He ran his hands over the machine, muttering to himself, completely ignoring the MMF with an indifference Rocío wished she could borrow. "It's still working! This is better than I hoped for..."

Rocío stepped away and ran her eyes over the rest of the room without seeing it, blindsided by the sudden clutch of rage and hate in her chest. There was nowhere to pace and nothing to punch and she couldn't throw evidence around. "Ancestors forget you, Hector Collins," she gritted out. If she'd had the inventor of the MMFs in front of her...she'd arrest him all over again. She wished she could scream, but she was a representative of Miraflores CJC and there were people around. One distracted inventor, but he counted. Plus whatever neighbors they hadn't seen.

"Hey." Hala raised a hand and then thought better of touching Rocío.

"I want to go to the Ka Empire and kill Hector Collins myself." She restrained the urge to kick an empty box.

"Hector Collins? Not Ariano?" Hala's voice, the same as always, even and non-judgmental, penetrated Rocío's rage. Hala wouldn't be surprised if Rocío told her the world was made of cheese. Though she'd demand evidence or at least Rocío's line of thought leading her to her conclusion.

The thought calmed Rocío and made it possible for her to reveal a horrible truth about herself. "Ariano couldn't have done this without Collins. One deranged man enabling the monomania of another." She met her partner's eyes and leaned forward, watching Hala as closely as she'd ever watched a suspect. The words climbed up her throat like bile. "Hala, we've arrested murderers and rapists, and I've never hated them like I hate Collins. I *hate* him."

Hala's face didn't change. No judgement. No condemnation. Just waiting for Rocío to finish.

"I've never hated anyone so much." Rocío cleared her throat. "I don't like that about myself," she finished in a less intense tone of voice.

Now Hala's face changed. That was compassion. And understanding. Self-recrimination? Her eyes held Rocío's like a lifeline. "Then you don't like that about me, either. I hate him, too, and it challenges my sense of self. I believe in law, community justice, reparations and rehabilitation, but I would have to fight not to kill him if he was in front of me." Her voice was flat and controlled, telling Rocío exactly how much Hala was holding back. As much as Rocío was.

As always, it was easier to see someone else and be kind than to treat yourself with that kindness. "We're only human?" Rocío felt her way into what she wanted to say, the rage subsiding more with the need to think. "And he did a terrible thing to us personally, to people we love, and people we don't even know, but are sworn to protect. It's natural to be angry, to hate him, but it's what we do with the feelings that matter." Her voice gained strength with her certainty. "We acted in accordance with our deepest beliefs about what justice is. What the law is. We turned Hector Collins over to the adjudicator and we did the same with Ariano Serafini."

"We hated but we acted correctly," Hala said, her voice regaining its natural intonations.

"Yes. Does that mean…? Is it really over?" Rocío felt lightheaded at the the thought. She cleared stuff off a bench and dropped onto it, letting the wall support her weight because she suddenly felt like she couldn't. Hala followed, her thigh warm comfort pressed along the length of Rocío's, and draped her arm around Rocío's shoulders. "Because it doesn't feel like it. That anger came out of nowhere. It still seems to be happening, here and here and here." Rocío touched her forehead, chest and stomach.

"I know. Me too. But it really is over." Hala picked up one of Rocío's hands and squeezed it. "It won't be so raw eventually," Hala said slowly. "It will get buried, under the millions of mundane details of life. What you're going to eat for breakfast. Do you really give a bitter bureaucrat a puppy?"

"What I'm going to wear to my parents' party." Rocío laughed and breathed away the pinched feeling in her throat and chest for the first time since the Sanblas chaski had appeared. Maybe since November and the first MMF attack. It wasn't just her muscles relaxing, but a hard knot of anxiety in her mind. Only now that it was loosening did she realize how constricted with dread she had felt for so long. She was aware of Finn opening the cabinet in the kitchen area, but couldn't quite muster up the energy to stop him. *In a minute.* "Do you think we should let it get buried? It seems like something we should expose to air and maybe spread around so it decomposes evenly, rather than sitting like a lump at the bottom of our minds."

"Like you're doing now?"

"I know I still duck every time a pigeon flies too close. I don't think that's going to stop any time soon."

"Well, pigeons. Anyone in their right mind tries to stay away from pigeons."

Finn opened the closet door. A tidal wave of paper and cardboard fell on his head. "Ah!" he shrieked, raising his arms to protect himself.

Rocío and Hala bolted to their feet.

"Are you okay?" Rocío asked. *I should have stopped him.* Her mind filled with visions of the paperwork she'd have to fill out if a witness was injured by evidence in an apartment he probably shouldn't technically be in. *I don't know if we even have forms for that.*

Finn hesitantly lowered his hands. He rubbed a spot on his head, his attention caught on the new mess at his feet. "I am. I'm glad you caught this guy, and not just because you got my cold box back. That's a different kind of poison." He toed the papers heaped around his feet: pamphlets and placards covered in anti-river folk propaganda. The *nicest* ones said "River scum doesn't belong in La Bene" and "Send river scum where they belong," with a skull and crossbones, just in case the reader thought they belonged in La Bene. The rest connected river folk with infection and contamination.

"Maybe I should destroy my prototype," Finn said. "It's tainted now. Used to further hate and terror."

Rocío paused with her mouth open, not sure how she wanted to argue against that.

"That's illogical," Hala said. "Even if a tool came from a tainted source, and I don't believe that is the case, it can still be used for good. In fact, if you feel there is some cosmic scale you need to balance out, you could argue that you *must* use it for good."

It was like Hala was reading Rocío's thoughts from yesterday about her own people skills and answering them. This was one emotional reaction she was not going to have here, so, in spite of the catch in her throat and slight roaring in her ears, she said cheerfully, "Besides, I want to invest in your machine. Just think: ice cream for everyone, any time."

CHAPTER 17

TWO WEEKS LATER, on the morning of her parents' party, rude knocking awakened Rocío. She untangled herself from Isis and yesterday's clothing, which had apparently spent the night in bed with them, and fumbled herself into a robe. Her door, when opened, revealed a teenage boy. Rocío squinted and then recognized her mother's gardener's assistant, who was sometimes pressed into delivering messages.

"Good morning Señorx Díaz," he said way too cheerfully, thrust a folded message into her hands and scampered away.

"What?" Isis stumbled into the living room. She rubbed at the impression of a button on her cheek.

"Message from my mother."

"Toss it and make me coffee. I still don't understand this new appliance," Isis said, dropping a kiss on Rocío's shoulder.

Rocío turned the message over in her hands. She didn't need to open it to know that it contained a summons from her mother for help with whatever dire emergency was going to just *ruin* their party. But for the moments before she opened it, she could pretend it wasn't going to wreck havoc on her schedule, her emotions or Isis's mood. It was too late for her own mood.

She ran her thumb under the seal, cracking off the wax and

catching it on the kitchen counter, already crowded with mail, tins of tea and last night's empty plates.

"You didn't," Isis accused and made a grab for the message.

Rocío fended her off with an elbow."Don't be so melodramatic, Isis, you knew I would. She needs me."

"Why are you so gullible about this?" Isis asked, ignoring the intentionally inflammatory bit about being melodramatic. "She doesn't need *you*, she needs to *control* you."

"I don't want to have this fight again."

"Then stop running to her every time she snaps her fingers."

"She's my mother," Rocío said through gritted teeth, trying to hold onto her calm.

"*Mother* doesn't have to equal manipulator."

"But it does in my case," Rocío shouted.

"If you can see that, why do you let her manipulate you?" Isis shouted back.

"Because that's what she is, and she's my mother"

"Oh!" Isis threw the coffee scoop on the floor. Luckily it was empty. "If only you could hear yourself the way I do. You say that as if it were a winning argument – but it's not, it's just a fact. You've given it that power over you."

She disappeared into the bedroom and reemerged with her clothing bundled in her arms.

"Isis, don't–"

"I'm exercising great restraint to not scream at you–you don't need any more of that. Your family does that already." She swept up her shoes. "And I'm *not* melodramatic." She banged the door behind her.

Isis probably would change in the communal bathroom, wouldn't she? Not parade through the streets in Rocío's second favorite silk robe with the gold and red dragons? Right?

Rocío had been looking forward to a good morning with Isis as counterweight to the party later. Instead, Isis was gone and her mother wanted her to find, she glanced down at the note in her hand, twelve matching champagne flutes, handblown of course. The thing that Isis didn't understand was that it was easier to do what her parents wanted.

Not that she ever did it well enough to satisfy them, but the tantrums and recriminations were usually shorter, and there was less crying from her mother and fewer pained exclamations from her father.

The door banged open again, framing Isis. She dropped her shoes and marched up, right into Rocío's space, until her eyes crossed trying to keep Isis's face in focus. Isis poked her in the stomach. "Get dressed. I'm not leaving you alone for a second today."

Happiness bubbled up inside Rocío and she didn't feel as weighted down as she had a moment ago.

"We're going for breakfast and then we'll go looking for moon dust or whatever it is your parents can't live without."

"Champagne flutes." Rocío offered the note.

"Because Constanza's doesn't have those." Isis took the note, dropped it to the floor and curled her fingers around Rocío's wrist, tugging her even closer, her body warm against Rocío's. Isis kissed her, her lips soft, infusing heat into Rocío. And strength. A decision crystalized in her mind. Could she do it? Was it worth it? Probably not, but for some reason that wasn't going to stop her.

Rocío pulled away in spite of Isis's faint noise of protest. "I'm not wearing it."

"You're not wearing it?" Isis asked muzzily.

"I'm not."

"What...? The dress. From your parents. You're not wearing it! Yes!" Isis swept her into a dance steps and they fluttered across the living room, laughing. "You need—"

"I have something to wear." Rocío pulled Isis to a stop. "I need you, though. I need a plan." *If I'm going to make it through the party.*

"Of course. What do you want me to do? I bet I could get a horse into Constanza's dining room, that would distract everyone from what you're wearing."

Rocío snorted a laugh through her nose, picturing it. One of the work horses from Isis's house? Heavy, solid and phlegmatic? Or one she rode for fun, high-spirited and not at all happy to attend a party? She shook the images away. "I hadn't thought of anything so drastic. More going out in a blaze of champagne and recriminations."

"No, no, no. No going out in a glaze of guilt—"

"Blaze—"

"*Glaze* of guilt," Isis said firmly, staring her down, and Rocío shifted uncomfortably. "See! I knew you were thinking it. Champagne, I can approve of. Guilt, I cannot. And recriminations from your brutish parents not so much."

"Isis," Rocío protested.

"No, I won't say another word against them. I don't want you to change your mind." She held up a forestalling hand. "Or a horse, though I'm sure it would be fun. Though not for the horse. Or about Hala, though I really think you should invite her. I'll be a part of *your* plan. Politicians have their road maps. Actors have their methods. Detectives have a favored approach. What is the plan of attack?"

"Not attack!"

"Defense then!"

Rocío couldn't help laughing, although doubt was already a hard ball in her stomach. *I shouldn't. I'm the savior of La Bene, at least according to the newspapers. I can wear my own perdido clothes to a party. I might need more than just Isis's support.* "Well...the first step of my plan is doughnuts. I've been craving Diana's ever since I indulged in a spot of bribery."

Isis laughed and leaned her forehead against Rocío's. "Sure, I'll stand in line at ungodly o'clock in the morning for a sugar rush."

Rocío stepped into Constanza's with Isis at her side. She was clothed not in the frothy, youthful, pastel concoction her parents had sent her but in a deceptively simple sleeveless red velvet wrap dress with a pleated ivory satin skirt starting just above her knees. It was an adult's dress, meant for a woman who knew what she liked and wasn't afraid to show it, though that was a little belied by her racing pulse, almost as fast as when she'd spotted the first MMF on Pilar's boat. She reached for a role to play to get her through this night. Her first thought was Cateline, the doomed heroine of the play of the same name, but she shook it off. Not tonight. Her favorite then, Angharad, from "Angharad's Ride," her favorite dance. That was a woman who did her duty but as *she* interpreted it, not as everyone around her told her to do it.

Next to her, Isis was magnificent in an amethyst robe with darker purple embroidery on the collar, waist and hem. Her arms were bare except for rose gold armbands with jaguar heads and emeralds for eyes. Rocío and Isis greeted people, commented on the floral arrangements of frilly red flowers and the candles augmenting the electric lighting and snagged glasses of champagne—not in the flutes they'd found that afternoon—as they reached the dance floor where people had congregated to talk. A band played background music softly. Isis leaned away to speak to someone and Rocío spotted her mother.

Their eyes met, Analicía's widening comically and her mouth opening in an 'O' of surprise. Rocío clutched Isis's arm with suddenly numb fingers. A jeweled jaguar head bruised her thumb. "This was a mistake." *Ancestors protect me.*

Her mother's eyes narrowed and she turned to Rocío's father, her mouth sharp on cutting words. Rocío could hear the soft words spiking her ear in her memory. *Look what our disgraceful daughter is doing now. She's so ungrateful. Why does she try to upset me? Why can't she be more like her brother?* Not that they would ever give Miguel such ill-fitting clothes. It was as if they could see him, but they couldn't see Rocío, only what they wanted her to be and what she wasn't because she had failed them, by leaving home, by not giving them grandchildren, by choosing professions that didn't advance their agenda to climb to the top of the social ladder in La Bene. And out loud they'd say *How exotic our daughter looks. You wouldn't have thought red would be her color at all, but children, you can't tell them anything these days. A good thing we have Miguel, our pride and joy.*

"They're going to make a scene," she whispered to Isis with numb lips. Xavier's face was turning red and Analicía's lips were so pinched they had almost disappeared.

I can't stand it. She was seven again, at her birthday. Her parents had unveiled a piano and introduced a teacher and the protest had fallen out of her mouth even though she already knew better. "But mamá, I asked for singing lessons. Not piano." She had bit her lip, her eyes burning, already knowing she wasn't going to get singing lessons.

Her mother's face had flushed. "Piano is better than singing. Anyone can sing but only educated people play the piano, darling, you want to be *educated* don't you? A credit to your family. Not common, not crass."

And all the family members crowding around, suffocating her, telling her how grateful she should be, how thoughtful and wise her parents were, how much she was going to love piano and it would make her forget all about singing. That year Miguel had gotten what he wanted, some kind of game, his desires and their parents' running in parallel, acceptable and encouraged.

Just like then, her knees felt like elastic bands with all the strength stripped out of them. She gripped Isis's arm harder, trying to feel anything besides panic.

Isis cupped her hand under Rocío's elbow and smiled at someone Rocío couldn't see. "Picture the horse I didn't smuggle in," Isis said quietly in her ear. "Hooves planted on the dance floor, scuffing that perfect surface. Any horse I smuggled into a party would have ribbons in her mane and tail and bells on her bridle. She'd snort, like she went to fancy parties every day and didn't think much of them."

The nonsense broke through Rocío's panic like nothing else could. Depend on Isis to know.

"Now that I think of it, I'd like to get fancy tack that matches my jewelry today, a jaguar on a horse. What do you think of that?"

Rocío couldn't, quite, smile. But Isis was ridiculous, and the panic receded a little more. Feeling came back into her fingers and knees. She managed to plaster a pleasant expression back on her face.

And then Isis's spouses bracketed Rocío's parents, stopping their inexorable march on Rocío. They pulled the Ministrx of Natural Resources into the conversation. Xavier turned away from Rocío, releasing her from his stare, and smiled ingratiatingly at the Ministrx. Analicía laughed and tucked her hand in Xavier's elbow.

The world seemed to rush back in on Rocío—people laughing and talking, the ching of glasses struck together, the guitarist picking out notes with her fingernails. "I could hug them."

"All part of the plan."

"You promised them hugs?" *It's working,* she thought giddily. *They're* supposed *to talk to people all night.* "We didn't discuss that."

"Do you begrudge my spouses hugs?"

"Never!"

She could see another ministrx, this one a close associate of Isis, congratulating her parents. Of course this was their party, everyone wanted to talk to them. They might not have a chance to talk to Rocío all night. And there went Rocío's chief—the titular chief—so incompetent half the CJC did his job or covered up his mistakes—but he had been invited because of his connections to the Dhavale family, not because he was her boss. The other day, Rocío had let drop her father's interest in mining, feeling she was aiming a fire hose with one hand.

Isis grinned at her and swiped two more glasses of champagne from a tray. "I know you're not going to enjoy the party, but you can at least enjoy our lovely little manipulation on the side of good. I love conniving for a good cause."

The word manipulation gave Rocío a hiccup of a qualm, but "good cause" and the memory of using her manipulation—very good personal skills—to save her city from MMFs overcame it. *As long as I keep questioning myself that it's really for the good, and not just my good.*

Her brother Miguel and his spouse Sebastian appeared in front of them. Two dapper, slim men in feathered kilts, all the colors of a peacock, and extremely white, flowing blouses.

"Oh, you little pearls, you got Ik-ho to do your clothes. You look divine," Isis said.

Rocío took a sip of champagne, the bubbles tickling her throat, and managed to chat with her brother, not even sure what she was saying. A waiter with a tray blocked her view of Analicía and Xavier. She leaned to the side, trying to track them, but Sebastian asked her a question. She took her attention off them for one minute, Isis laughing at something Miguel said, and Analicía appeared at her elbow. Xavier frowned behind her, chewing on his mustache.

Rocío froze, her mind blank.

"Rocío, how could you? What are you—"

Isis's eyes widened, the kohl making them look even darker and more enchanting than ever, and then her stage trained voice easily overwhelmed Analicía's. "Señorx! Here is the happy couple now! Congratulations on your new contract and anniversary! You look ravishing. And you, señorx, so handsome. Miguel takes after you."

"Ministrx Soler," Xavier said to Isis, "thank you. So kind. Thank you for coming. But I need to talk to R—"

"Yes, of course. It's time for a toast." Isis waved at the band and they played a fanfare.

"What an honor." Analicía's smile looked like it would cut her own cheeks, but she didn't know whether to glare at Rocío or simper at Isis.

"To the happy couple! May they have as many years of happiness ahead of them as they have behind them." Isis raised her champagne glass and took a sip.

"Thank you, Ministrx, so kind," Xavier said. "Now, Rocío—"

"I have a toast." Rocío's voice came out muted, but Isis waved at the band and they played another flourish. The crowd circled around them, smiling, with drinks half raised in anticipation. *Surely this should be the easiest crowd to handle? After angry dockworkers, angry river folk and angry Benerex?*

"Rocío?" Isis asked.

"To Analicía and Xavier," Rocío said, her voice gaining strength, "who got what they deserve—" *whoops that came out more naked than I intended*— "decades of enduring love and in—affection and each other." *Seres celestiales, what is wrong with me?* People clapped, not hearing the slip or the strain in her voice.

Analicía had two red spots high on her cheeks and Xavier's mustache bristled. "Daughter—"

Not good. So much for my plan. She said the first thing that came into her head to delay the inevitable. "To share that affection, they invite you all to join them in their season box at [name] fields, my gift to them."

People, clapped harder, exclaimed in surprise and enthusiasm, and surrounded her parents to enthuse over such a wonderful gift.

"Pato?!" Miguel said, half laughed, half sounded horrified. "They hate pato!" It was the one social event their parents avoided, no matter how many Benerex elite gathered to enjoy the game. They disdained the crowds, the horses, the sun, the violence…everything about it.

"It's Isis's fault—all I could think of were horses!"

"You haven't even bought the box?" Miguel dissolved into laughter. He grabbed onto his spouse to stay upright as he howled, clutching his stomach. Sebastian started to smile.

Isis was already grinning. "That was some toast." She saluted Rocío with her glass and drained her champagne.

"No, I haven't—Isis, Miguel, you have to help me! What did I do?"

What she had done was keep her parents away from her all night. Their guests made a solid wall between them and Rocío as they enthused about pato, shared their best stories or asked for a seat in their box.

EPILOGUE

"Congratulations!"

Everyone in Miraflores CJC stood up, cheering and clapping, as Rocío and Hala entered the office. Several advocates threw confetti into the air. Chaskis had run ahead with the verdict in Ariano Serafini's adjudication: guilty. Sentenced to hard labor as part of the convict exchange program with the Ka Empire to the south. He would spend the rest of his life working in a mine or building roads or terracing previously unused land for farms high in the Cordillera del sur, cut off from his native Benerex magic and only slowly, if ever, gaining the skill to use the magic of the Ka Empire.

"Three cheers for Hala and Rocío!" someone shouted.

Her fellow advocates clapped them on their backs, shook their hands and generally expressed their relief that it was all over. Rocío smiled and made the appropriate responses. She *was* glad, but usually at this point she buzzed with a sense of a job well done—and it was strange that in such an important case, she felt flat and tired.

After a while, the tea and cakes were consumed, and everyone calmed down and turned back to their cases and files. The usual low hum of conversations and activity filled the big room.

"Are you okay?" Hala asked quietly, raising an eyebrow.

Rocío sighed and sat on the edge of her desk. "I don't like the convict exchange program."

"What, not even for terrible criminals like Ariano Serafini?"

"Our whole system of justice is based on the idea of healing people, communities and perpetrators as a way to stop crime. This doesn't feel like that. It feels like punishment."

"So you want Ariano to suffer internally, not externally?" Hala said.

Rocío snorted a laugh. "Okay, yes. But you know I'm right. Hard labor isn't going to teach him empathy. It's going to harden his resentment."

"I know. But community justice works best at the local level. Our system isn't equipped to deal with crimes of this magnitude, against the entire city, so it isn't surprising that it failed in some ways in this case. But." Hala tapped her foot on Rocío's, part *pay attention*, part *I'm here, too.* "Pilar is safe now. Her children are safe. She got to tell Ariano what he did to her and what she felt without fear of retribution. Her children got to see that their father isn't going to be able to hurt them anymore. That's a kind of justice and healing. Sometimes that's the justice we get. And he will have a chance at rehabilitation in the Ka Empire. Not as good a one as here, but still a chance."

Rocío picked up the picture of her nonna and rubbed dust off the frame. "I know. Usually I find the adjudication process invigorating. All those people getting their say and deciding how to move forward. This time I was just exhausted."

"This case was a little too close to home?"

Rocío put down the photo with a click. "I don't know what you're talking about. What are we working on next?"

"Hmm."

"Don't hmm me."

"I have a message from the superintendent of the Miraflores subterranean train line."

"What you can't say subte like the rest of us?"

Hala grinned at her, and Rocío realized she'd done it on purpose to lighten the mood.

"We also have—"

"Don't tell me, a livestock complaint."

"In a way."

"What does that mean?" Rocío squinted suspiciously at her partner.

"We have a complaint about someone keeping crocodiles in their rain reservoir and the crocodiles escaping."

"A crocodile complaint? Are you kidding?"

"I'm not—"

One of the chaskis popped up at Hala's side. "There's someone to see you here from Cempol," Khadija said, tilting her head at a woman standing in the doorway.

The woman was pale and tall, with light brown hair, and an aggressive stance. Her voice echoed through the big room. "I'm Officer Smith from Cempol. I'm looking for Haddad and Díaz."

"She couldn't wait?" Khadija sniffed and faded out of sight.

One of the other advocates pointed them out, and Officer Smith stumped over to them.

Rocío moved to stand shoulder to shoulder with her partner and felt Hala bristle at the omission of their titles. Rocío would expect that familiarity from a colleague, but from someone she'd never met it felt like an insult.

"I'm Detective Haddad, and this is Detective Díaz."

"What can we do for Cempol today?" Rocío asked, automatically assuming the sweet tones she used with intransigent bureaucrats.

"I have forms H308 and GB18 for you to fill out."

"Pursuant to what?"

Smith consulted the folder tab. "Case 49-587. H308 is for the transfer of evidence—"

"I know what the forms are," Hala said. "What evidence are you here to collect? That's a Cempol case number, not a Miraflores one."

"The biological evidence in the Ariano Serafini case."

"The biological..." Hala looked at Rocío, who shrugged.

"The biological evidence," Officer Smith repeated.

"Officer Smith, there is no biological evidence," Rocío said carefully, as if she spoke to someone whose command of Benerex wasn't too strong. "It was imported magic, and imported magic dissolves.

Poof." Rocío repeated Trinidad's gesture, raising her hand and flicking her fingers open.

"There are photographs," Hala added when Smith didn't respond.

"Photographs are an unacceptable substitute for the biological evidence. Only biological evidence can be stored in the category 'Biological evidence.'" She thrust the forms at them again. Neither of them reached for them. "I need you to fill these out and surrender the biological evidence in the Serafini case."

"Officer Smith, I just told you there is no evidence, not any more."

"You're being obstructionist. I'm giving you—"

"Excuse me—"

"—one last chance and then I'm reporting you to your chief."

Behind Smith's back, Khadija rolled her eyes.

"Go ahead," Rocío said, hanging onto her patience. "The deputy chief is on the third floor. The chief isn't here today." The deputy chief, unlike the chief, was infinitely competent. If anyone could sort out a self-righteous Cempol bureaucrat with blinders on, it was the deputy chief.

Smith wheeled away and marched to the stairs like she had the proverbial stick up her ass.

Rocío waited until she was out of sight to sag against her desk. "Whew. As my nonna used to say, what a piece of work."

"I concur," Hala said.

"I'm going to make sure she doesn't start looking for evidence on her own." Khadija flounced off.

"Eavesdrop, she means," Rocío said.

Hala drummed her fingers on the back of her chair. "I do hope we don't have to deal with her again."

"Oh, don't say that." Rocío flicked her fingers in an avert gesture. "Now you've jinxed it. We're going to see her everywhere."

"Have not."

"What are you twelve?" The normalcy of squabbling with Hala settled around her, and her spirits lifted. *It really is over—no more MMFs. And we can let that fear go?* she wondered tentatively. Rocío took an unconstricted breath and then another, more of the heaviness lifting. She grinned at her partner and Hala smiled back.

～

Want to read more about Rocío and Hala? Their next adventure starts with a newly discovered crypt in the subway, a missing choreographer, and reports of impossible magic. Turn the page for an excerpt from **Shadow of the City.**

Subscribe to R. Morgan's awesome newsletter for exclusive bonus content, including the short story, "A Case of Fear," where Rocío and Hala investigate art vandalism at a newfangled thing called an "art gallery", and updates on upcoming books.

Sign up at www.rafmorgan.com.

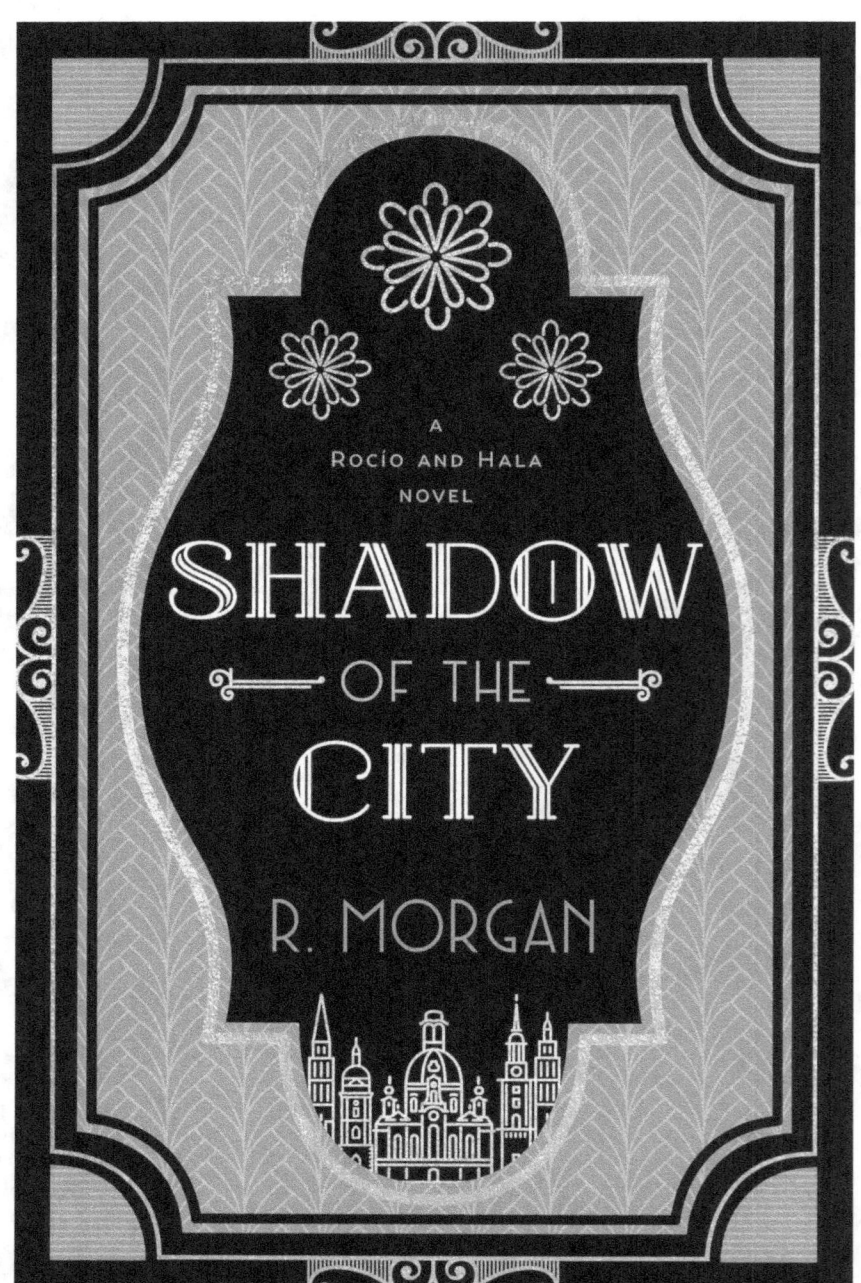

A
Rocío and Hala
NOVEL

SHADOW
OF THE
CITY

R. MORGAN

CHAPTER 1

D<small>ETECTIVE</small> R<small>OCÍO</small> D<small>ÍAZ</small> R<small>OSSI</small> had investigated a lot of crimes in her seven years with Miraflores Community Justice Center, but none had ever involved an underground access tunnel to the subte, a disappearing wall, and an empty room that resembled a crypt.

"Hala, we're supposed to be determining how the wall could be removed without anyone noticing, not investigating the room that appeared once the wall was gone," Rocío reminded her partner, Detective Hala Haddad Sosa. "Not that disappearing walls or empty rooms are crimes. I'm not even sure what we're doing here."

Her voice rang overloud off the close, pitted brick walls and vaulted ceiling, betraying her nerves. Behind her, electric bulbs, retrofitted into wrought-iron brackets for gaslights, lit the access tunnel for the subte—the subterranean train. Even here, twenty meters below the city, the lights had amber-tinted glass shades.

Only Rocío's flashlight lit the room before her, small and dusty and claustrophobic. Clearly it was not part of the subte—even further out of their jurisdiction than she had thought. And creepier. She hated anything having to do with old burials, long-dead bodies or strange funeral practices, a legacy of her nonna, who had liked bloodcurdling cautionary tales, especially ones about the Ghost Years. The low platform in the middle of the room was perfect for a coffin and made Rocío think of all those stories. Luckily the few bodies she saw as a detective were generally recently dead.

The flashlight in her hand flickered and died, and Rocío's breath hitched.

"The empty room might logically have something to do with the missing wall. The light, please," Hala said, steady and reassuring as always.

Rocío shook the flashlight to see if the connection was loose. "It's dead, just a sec."

She recharged the battery with the innate magic every Benerex had, a process a bit like pushing a button that existed only in her mind. The flashlight flickered back to life, and she pointed it over Hala's shoulder, catching her cropped black hair and dark skin in its jittery beam before sweeping it across the nonexistent, noncriminal contents.

"Go back to the plinth in the center," Hala said.

Rocío made a face but obeyed. "What do you see?" She steadied the light. The plinth was about four centimeters high, dust-grimed blue, unadorned and empty. "I see the tracks of at least two people besides us, though I can't tell if they were here this morning or two centuries ago."

The air smelled of machine oil and magic—like ozone and burnt sugar—most likely from the batteries powering the lights in the tunnel. They'd passed the battery room on the way here, one of the many 'landmarks' Old Nico had mentioned in his directions to supplement the signage on the walls. Old Nico was a neighborhood institution and had been the superintendent for this section of the Miraflores subte line for almost as long as it had been here, through flooding, strikes and storms. A few months ago, he had tipped them off about tainted cacao beans being smuggled through the subte tunnels, so when he had flagged them down from his booth and asked for help, they had agreed to check out the missing wall and apply their expertise to the mystery.

"Not two centuries." Hala crouched for a better view of the floor, and Rocío adjusted the flashlight. After seven years of working together, some things were second nature. "A little more to the right.

Look how the footprints smudge this thicker dust on the threshold. They entered and exited from this tunnel, which was only possible sometime in the last week or so, according to Old Nico."

She didn't say anything about Rocío missing the obvious. For one thing, what was obvious to Hala was not always obvious to anyone else. And after seven years of friendship, she knew a thing or two about Rocío, including the fear of ghosts that was distracting her now. Instead Hala reached up and guided Rocío's hand and the flashlight beam to the opposite wall, revealing a bricked-up doorway in the stone. Her hand was warm and dry on Rocío's. She stopped at a maker's stamp on one of the bricks. The upside-down logo wasn't familiar to Rocío.

"Ah, that's González and González, an Iberex brickwork that went out of business two hundred years ago. The brick must have been ballast in a trading ship, which means it's likely that other door, and this room, predate the subte by at least as long."

Of course Hala knew that. "Unless someone reused old bricks."

"Yes." Hala pointed Rocío's flashlight at the other two walls, each with its own bricked-up doorway, and then at the wall immediately to their left. "Look at that."

In Rocío's imagination, the darkness immediately populated itself with ghosts and bogeymen. She squelched those thoughts firmly. "With everything you carry in your pockets, I don't understand why you refuse to carry a flashlight."

Hala always wore sturdy broadcloth trousers covered in pockets of disparate sizes, widths and uses, from which she routinely extracted astonishingly varied things, such as mosquito repellant or samples of first-century silk from Jeen. The invariable trousers necessitated a thick leather belt to hold them up, but she varied her tops; today it was a flannel work shirt in her favorite green and a woolen overcoat. Rocío's trousers had a more normal number of pockets, and her alpaca wool sweater and camel hair coat would have done a good job of keeping her warm if the chill hadn't originated from inside her. With her long dark hair wound up and pinned, the nape of her neck felt exposed. She should have worn a scarf.

"You barely carry anything—it's only fair. Look." Hala pointed to a dark patch on the newly exposed stone.

"You still haven't answered my question. What are we doing here?"

"Hold the light steady." Hala used tweezers to free a splinter, dropped it into an evidence bag and returned everything to yet another pocket. "This room wasn't empty. The corner of one of the tiles is chipped, and whoever was here removed something wooden. I want forensics." She stood, dusted off her knees and pushed her bangs to the side. They were long for Hala, and she would no doubt raze them back to infinitesimal soon.

"Property crimes," Rocío said dubiously, "are not our office. And are too bougie for your interest even if they were. We should have told Old Nico to contact POPA." POPA was the disordered acronym for Property Offenses Against the People.

"And let him down? You wouldn't."

Rocío blew out her breath in surrender. "Okay, I wouldn't. But we should get someone from POPA here instead. That should satisfy Old Nico. I don't want to come back down here with forensics." She shuddered theatrically. "I think we deserve pastries from Benito's after this."

"I'm surprised at you," Hala said, removing her spectacles and stowing them in a case in another pocket. "Old Nico deserves better from us. If he hadn't told us the last time he saw something strange, we never would have found out who was smuggling those cacao beans. And what's stranger than almost two hundred kilos of stone going missing without anyone noticing?"

Rocío refused to be distracted by Hala's off-the-cuff estimation. Sudden suspicion stabbed through her. "Let me guess." She swung the light to shine on Hala's face.

Hala blinked back at her, her expression completely blank, a definite sign of no good.

"'Anything interesting, you tell me, Old Nico, and we'll investigate for you,'" Rocío said, imitating Hala's even voice. "That's what you told him, isn't it? Seres celestiales—you and your curiosity. Fine. Let's go talk to Old Nico about when this could have happened, and then tube forensics. Just let me out of here."

∼

Consulting with Old Nico again revealed that the window, so to speak, for his disappearing wall had to be between Saturday, 4 April and today, Tuesday, 14 April. The old man extracted a willing promise from Hala to follow up with the Department of Transportation about work orders while he investigated whether anyone had lost a key to the maintenance entrances; those were the least conspicuous ways to remove such a quantity of rock.

Leaving Old Nico's office, Rocío and Hala traversed the bowels of the city via more access tunnels and very civilized stairs, neither of which resembled actual bowels, thank the seres celestiales, and emerged, blinking, outside. Rocío opened her umbrella and took a deep breath of leaf mold and horse manure. The muscles in her back relaxed, and thoughts of ghosts receded to where they belonged, the dim recesses of her mind.

In mid-autumn, the city of La Beneficia de nuestros vecinos y los seres celestiales (La Bene for short) was not at her most attractive, but the rain pattered softly, comfortingly, and birds cheeped slightly frantically, as if they had stayed out late partying instead of doing their housekeeping chores for the winter and now realized how unprepared they were. On the median, the brightly colored umbrellas of pedestrians waiting for a horse-drawn trolley to pass made a pleasant picture against the bare branches of the tipa trees lining the broad avenue.

Hala turned left on 15 de agosto instead of right towards the tube office. Rocío ambled after her and popped a piece of gum into her mouth, waiting to see if Hala was going to tell her where they were going now. Rocío absently greeted a street cleaner she knew and a neighbor from her apartment building, which was only a few blocks away, where the neighborhood changed from swank to merely chic.

"I wish someone had invented recording more than ten years ago so we had an idea what the really old accents sounded like." Hala turned left on Calle ch'eju'ut, one of the oldest streets in the city, where families who traced their ancestry to the first refugees to arrive in La Bene lived in mansions behind more trees, whitewashed walls and wrought-iron gates.

Rocío accepted this non sequitur with the ease of practice. "Like Old Nico's? My grandparents sounded like him, except for my nonna, of course. Are you thinking of doing a linguistic analysis?"

"I'd love to track how fast each immigrant group adapts to and changes the dominant accent."

"So where are we going?" Rocío finally gave in and asked.

Hala stopped abruptly at the entrance to the biggest house on the street. The black gates were worked in the shape of mountain peaks tipped with gold. Rocío tilted her umbrella back to get a better look at the grounds and the mansion, though she could see only a slice of dark green manicured oleander bushes and a white portico and columns.

"Montenegro House," Hala said. "If it's not above the underground room, I'll eat my socks."

"Don't do that. You're still wearing yesterday's."

Hala turned her intense stare from the house to Rocío. "How do you know that?"

It was a game they played; their minds worked so differently that they often came to the same conclusion by wildly different routes. But that didn't mean Rocío couldn't get back at Hala a bit for luring her underground and not telling her where they were going after.

"Really, Hala? I *am* a detective. A bona fide member of the Miraflores Community Justice Center. And I happen to know you only have one pair of $E=mc^2$ socks. Which you also wore yesterday. And laundry day is Sunday in your house."

"Umphf. I ran out of clean socks because of the rain on Tuesday."

"Hala, it *is* Tuesday."

"Last Tuesday. I missed laundry entirely this week." She turned back to the house. "Rocío, the empty room is there. What's more, it must be within their wards."

"You're sure?" Rocío asked, straightening.

"Dirty socks sure."

"About the wards, too? Because opening up an unused room in the subte is one thing, but getting through expensive wards like the Montenegros must have is another."

"Yes."

Her flat tone increased Rocío's worry. "Surely we'd have heard if someone had tampered with their wards."

Then again, the Montenegros, one of the wealthiest and most important families in the city, had their fingers in most political pies. So maybe not.

"They might not know yet." Hala marched up to the gate.

"Wait."

Hala had people skills; she just didn't always use them. She showed her ID booklet to the gatekeeper.

"Let me do the talking," Rocío whispered. "They're not going to like this."

"I usually do."

The gatekeeper gave them a nod and allowed them in, revealing the house at the end of the drive. Black gate, white shell drive, white house, black angular details around the door and windows. It reminded Rocío of the Kaellic dance troupe that had come through last year, their bodies stiff straight lines imposed on the world, emphasized by the stark white costumes printed with black knotwork designs.

As they approached, the door opened, disgorging the Ministrx of External Relations—an imposing older man with silver hair—and two women in their early thirties, who looked enough alike to be cousins and were probably assistants. All three were most likely related, because that's how politics worked in La Bene. The pins in their elaborately arranged hair were no doubt real gold and silver with real gemstones, unlike Rocío's enameled silver-plated steel. The woman with the lighter brown hair whispered to the others, recognition and interest flaring in her eyes, and Rocío braced herself.

Ministrx O'Higgins nodded courteously. "Detectives, is there a problem?"

"Nothing to worry about," Rocío said blithely.

"I'm Ministrx O'Higgins Cruz, and these are my assistants,

Gumersinda de Herrera Nuñes and Críspula de Herrera Carmona. Should we be concerned for Ministrx Montenegro?"

As a stratagem to extract Rocío's and Hala's names, it was fairly obvious.

"Not at all, ministrx," Hala said. "Have a good day."

Rocío guessed that as soon as the group stepped past the gate, they would begin to speculate wildly. That wouldn't endear them to Ministrx Montenegro when she learned of it.

When they were out of earshot, Rocío said, "Those are unfortunate names."

"Very old Benerex names. The twenty-fourth of November and the thirteenth of March in the old almanac," Hala said, reprising her role as human repository of mostly forgotten facts.

"Ah, of course," Rocío said dryly, used to Hala's habit of spouting obscure information.

The Montenegros' majordomo held the door open without communicating any welcome. She was middle-aged, with the straight nose and sharp cheekbones of Disi ancestry. The laugh lines around her eyes hinted at a sense of humor that was not in evidence at the moment. She didn't blink when Hala introduced them, and she didn't offer to take their coats or umbrellas.

"Ministrx Montenegro is not available at the moment."

Rocío nudged Hala out of the way. "We understand the ministrx is a busy woman," she said, balancing courtesy and authority. "We only need a moment to speak with her. It is important and sensitive. I'm sure she would like to hear what we have to say."

"The ministrx is unable to see you at this time."

"Tell her—"

Rocío stepped on Hala's foot and spoke over her. "We would like to leave her a note."

"Of course." The majordomo extracted the necessary tools from the table in the foyer and continued to block further entry to the house, so Rocío penned her note in situ, summing up the situation, and folded it.

"We'll wait, just in case," Rocío said.

The majordomo withdrew up the stairs and left them dripping on the black-and-white mosaic inlay.

"I don't see how that was more effective than what I was going to say," Hala said. She flicked a nail against the cobalt vase on the silver-mounted demilune table, and it pinged.

"Don't do that," Rocío said. "It's worth your yearly salary."

Hala hesitated with her hand still raised and gave Rocío an incredulous look.

"Seriously. It depends on what your goal is," Rocío said. "Mine is primarily to not offend the ministrx so much she decides to get us fired and only secondarily to let her know she might have a problem."

Hala snorted. The majordomo's return precluded any further response, for which Rocío was grateful.

"The ministrx is not available."

"Thank you." Rocío nodded to her and pulled Hala out the door by her arm. At least it had stopped raining. Hala didn't speak as they crunched down the drive to the street.

"What do you think?" Hala asked, turning the right way for the tube office.

"You know as well as I do that interpreting body language depends on each individual's patterns, and changes to the pattern—"

"Rocío."

"If you'd let me finish, I was going to say that the majordomo seemed more surprised on her return than she was to see us knocking on the door, so you could extrapolate that she read the note or passed it on to the ministrx, with the same result in either case."

"Will the ministrx call us back?"

Rocío's parents had spent decades aspiring to leave the ranks of the well heeled and well bred to join the highest ranks of the political elite of La Bene, and had ... bestowed ... upon Rocío all the education and exposure money could buy in an effort to achieve that goal. At seventeen, Rocío had run away to join the theater. At thirty-four, she had joined the CJC. In neither career had she been able to prove her parents entirely wrong; knowledge of the elite was useful.

"I think she will. Eventually."

Plaza de los mártires, a trapezoid-shaped plaza left from when the city was part of the Ka Empire, was deserted because of the recent rain, except for a man feeding quail next to the DON'T FEED THE BIRDS sign. Rocío felt free to ignore the violation of the public good, especially as no one had complained about it to her. On the west side, the tube office stood two doors down from the Community Justice Center in a row of shops, cafes and homes, the buildings low shapes that at any other time of the year emphasized the largeness of the sky; in autumn they seemed to barely hold it up.

This pneumatic tube office wasn't open to the general public but was reserved for the use of public servants such as bona fide members of the Miraflores Community Justice Center. Such as them. Also, firefighters and emergency workers of all types. Rocío pushed open the heavy wooden door. Gustavo, the big, dark-skinned magicker in charge of the office, had his feet up and a cup of cafe con leche cradled in his lap. It smelled heavenly and was probably from Benito's. Rocío shot an accusing look at Hala, who ignored her.

Gustavo lowered his feet with a thump and rubbed the back of his hand against his tightly curling beard. "This doesn't look like an emergency. I barely recognize you, Rocío, in this state of calm."

"I'm calm."

"She's calm." He turned his thumb at Hala.

"She's dead inside," Rocío joked.

"I'm rational, which both of you could be if you only tried," Hala said.

When Rocío had joined the CJC, it had taken almost six months to figure out if Hala had a sense of humor and how to tell when she was joking. The answer was yes, and the corner of her left eye crinkled a bit. It barely crinkled now. Only a few other masters of the human face and a retired actor turned detective who had received conditional love from her parents would have noticed.

"What is it this time?" Gustavo asked. "I haven't recovered from the outbreak of malarial mosquito fairies four months ago."

"Technically you'd be dead if you hadn't recovered from the MMFs," Hala said. "We all would be."

Rocío shuddered at the memory of the demented fairy faces on mosquitos the size of cicada wasps. She had scars on her hands from their bites, and quick-onset malaria hadn't been fun either, but they'd caught the man responsible. The city adjudicator had found no signs of remorse in him, and the people of La Bene had almost unanimously asked for transportation, and so he had been sent to the Ka Empire to the south. Because magic was geographic in nature—the manipulation of electrical energy in La Bene or the manipulation of fairies in Enkladt, to name just two—he would have to relearn how to use magic, which the Ka shamans would prevent.

"Not an emergency," Rocío said. "Just a message. A routine, unimportant message."

"Uh-huh." Gustavo didn't look like he believed her. She didn't believe herself, either. Hala had a talent for discovering the strange, and Rocío was developing a talent for the dangerous. The combination often had unnerving results.

They trooped down into the bowels of the earth again—though compared to the subte, these bowels were too short for viability for a living organism—and entered a well-lit, civilized office. Or rather a well-lit cross between the office of a low-level bureaucrat and a child's idea of a mad scientist magicker's den constructed by a master artisan, which it kind of was.

Bins marked with dates lined the bottom edges of all four walls, logbooks peeking out of the tops of a few. Above them were the end points of the pneumatic tubes through which messages in rocket-shaped capsules hurtled across La Bene in minutes to each district's community justice center, public tube office, fire station, or the House of Refuges, La Bene's seat of government. In the center of the room was the power apparatus, made of gleaming steel and copper and bearing more than a passing resemblance to a grasshopper as long as Rocío's arm. It needed a level-three magicker to operate, hence Gustavo.

Hala seized a pad of very thin paper and a pen from Gustavo's desk, pushed aside machine parts and more pads, and started scribbling.

"They'll never be able to read that," Rocío said, looking over Hala's shoulder. Hala crumpled her first effort and started again. "Better ask if there was any work done that Old Nico might not know about."

Hala stopped writing to give her an incredulous look.

"Okay, probably not, but just ask."

"Where to?" Gustavo asked.

"Department of Transportation," Rocío and Hala said at the same time.

"Well, as long as you're sure." Gustavo winked at Rocío. "Don't forget to date it."

Hala dated it in the three calendars—La Bene's: 14 April, year 449; the Ya Empire's: 12.14.15.14.13 / 2 Ben / 11 kumk'u / Lord of the Night G5; and the Ka Empire's: Year 17 of the Divine Emperor Lloque.

"Show-off," Rocío said. Most people needed a calendar converter for the Ya Empire's system.

Hala's eye crinkled a bit more.

Gustavo rummaged in yet another bin, producing one of the dull brown rocket capsules, since it wasn't an emergency. Those got red capsules for fire, green for medical assistance, yellow for community justice advocates, et cetera. In spite of all the emergencies Rocío had dealt with, she still occasionally had the impulse to manufacture one so she could enjoy launching the shiny capsules into the tubes.

Hala jammed her now-legible note inside the capsule, and Gustavo flipped the switch on the grasshopper machine, keeping his other hand on the contact panel on its back to power it with his magic. The machine purred, a disconcertingly catlike sound to come from a hard-edged, shiny grasshopper-like machine, powering the hidden pump that sucked air through the tubes.

In La Bene magic manifested as electrical energy, an extension of the body's electric field beyond its bounds and under conscious control. In school everyone learned to warm their tea and not give others accidental electrical shocks. Those who went to the University for magic learned more. The CJC's basic certificate program ensured advocates learned to detect residual magical fields and work some specialized machinery. Rocío had passed, barely, because magical foundational theory was hard, and you couldn't practice more advanced magic without it. Others, like Gustavo, went to the University and became bureaucrats or teachers or engineers who developed new machines. Anyone could, just like anyone could become a plumber, but not everyone wanted to become a magicker, just like not everyone wanted to be a plumber.

Gustavo cocked his head, his gaze turned inward, barely looking at the gauge that measured magical input into the machine. He didn't need to; he'd been the tube magicker here for longer than Rocío had been a detective.

"Tube fifty-two," he said, which wasn't magic at all but mechanics.

Hala opened the cap on the indicated tube and tossed the capsule inside. The vacuum sucked it away.

CHAPTER 2

THE COMMUNITY JUSTICE CENTER was a graceful old house that had been donated to the CJC around the same time the subte had been built. It dated back almost to the founding of La Bene and the arrival of the first refugees more than four hundred years ago. The previous owner still maintained the pristine white façade, the crisp molded scrolls and seashells above the door and windows, and the polished brass doorknob. The wooden shutters in the deep-set windows were open, allowing in as much light as possible on such a dim day and letting out the sounds of yelling.

Rocío and Hala exchanged a glance and stepped inside, into a raucous wave of sound.

Three teenagers in the rumpled school sarongs and sweaters of the Hakaara Polytechnic School sullenly kicked their heels against the legs of the bench on the left, waiting for a counselor to help them sort out their problem. A woman in a Ya-style indigo huipil with a long-sleeved black shirt underneath and a man in a black house servant cap and an unseasonable kilt stood at the desk across from the door, loudly arguing about who had arrived first.

Chief Maurata Martínez, in a sadly precedented display, was babbling about a hole puncher and blocking the stairs, while at the bottom, Deputy Chief Oshinsky bas Rifke huddled with her assistant and two jurisprudence adjudicators. And two chaskis—teenaged message runners serving vocational apprenticeships with the CJC in the hopes of getting adult jobs there as advocates, support staff, counselors, magickers or forensic techs—were betting on the reason for Maurata's upset.

Advocate Espinoza Onyeneme, who should have been at the desk, pounced on Rocío and Hala before the door even closed behind them. "Someone to see you," she shouted, her next words lost as the teenagers erupted in an argument about who had sabotaged whom in the mathematics competition.

Chief Maurata, who should have asserted control in the CJC, had never really twigged to the fact that it was part of his responsibilities. Deputy Chief Oshinsky usually did his job as well as her own, but her discussion seemed serious. Which left Maurata's job, as usual, to anyone who stepped into his vacuum.

"Enough!" Rocío's stage-trained shout stunned everyone into silence. "Chief Maurata, the hole puncher is in the second office on the left on the third floor."

He bolted up the stairs as if the future of the CJC depended on it.

"You"—she pointed her finger at the three kids—"will shut up, or we'll tell the adjudicator you should all get double community service sorting garbage."

One of the girls said, "That's not—"

The other one pinched her, and she stopped talking.

Rocío folded her arms and stared them down. They ducked their heads, whispering, and gave her dirty looks, but since they had quieted, Rocío ignored them.

Now that Maurata was no longer blocking the way, Deputy Chief Oshinsky hustled her group up the stairs.

Hala took over. "Officer Espinoza, Ministrx Montenegro may be contacting us soon about a crime. I want to hear about it when she does. And we're expecting a return message from the Department of Transportation."

"Are you predicting crimes now?" Espinoza asked incredulously. "Never mind. Detective Díaz, thank you for getting them to listen."

Espinoza was the shortest person Rocío had ever known, though she compensated by staying extremely fit, taking up more room than could be accounted for physically, and sporting a serious expression, but she probably hadn't loomed over the teenagers convincingly enough. She saved that for adults who should have known better than to do whatever had landed them at the CJC. Also, she was still recovering from gender-affirming surgery, which was why she was on desk duty on a Tuesday, a time that generally didn't require much looming.

"There's a chaski for you in interview three. She has a message from your mother," Espinoza said.

Hala had started to turn away, but she stopped to listen.

Stiffening, Rocío fiddled with a hairpin that didn't need fixing. An automatic soothing habit. She forced her hand down. "I could just ignore her."

"You could," Hala said.

"I was *joking*," Rocío said, half offended Hala could think she was serious.

"Sadly, I knew that."

Rocío caught Espinoza's eye and tilted her head at the teenagers, who were muttering again. Espinoza nodded and pointed the woman in the huipil to a seat; she huffed and plopped into it with as much attitude as the teenagers. Espinoza rolled her eyes and herded the kids to a counselor's office.

Hala trailed Rocío to interview three, which was the nicest, the one with the comfortable furniture and watercolor paintings of fishing boats. The chaski, a young woman in loose pants and a tight jacket, jumped up when Rocío entered the room. Hala leaned against the doorway, radiating disapproval.

"Are you Rocío Díaz Rossi?" the chaski asked. At Rocío's nod, the chaski tapped the badge of the tube office pinned to her jacket. "Message for you from Analicía Rossi Dey." She handed Rocío an elaborately folded and sealed letter.

Rocío cracked the seal over the table to catch the pieces of wax. It was the usual summons. She stifled a disgusted sigh. It would just give Hala ammunition she didn't need.

"No response," she told the chaski, who bobbed her head and scampered out of the room.

"You're going?" Hala asked, so studiously neutral it called to mind every comment she'd ever made on the subject of Rocío's inconsiderate, exhausting mother.

"She said it's urgent." Rocío matched Hala's tone to avoid discussion. Hala couldn't understand; her family was different. Lucky, lucky Hala.

"Just once, you could not go," Hala said.

"I know you don't like her, but she's my mother," Rocío explained, gesturing inadequately. "I'll be back soon."

~

On her way back to the CJC, Rocío wrote summonses for a woman scalping opera tickets and a food vendor whose health inspection sticker had expired, but it didn't make her feel better. She wanted to arrest a bad guy, preferably someone who mugged little old ladies or a corrupt politician or her mother, for the crime of terminal delusion. She'd invent the category just for her. If she slipped the paperwork into Maurata's expense reports, he might sign it without noticing.

Assistant. That's what she thinks I'm worth. The summons had been an ambush, her mother's minor politician friend offering her a job as an assistant. As if she didn't already have a job, and one she liked.

"Don't be silly—that job doesn't matter, darling. The CJC is just the district government. It isn't real government," her mother had said, making *darling* sound more like an epithet than an endearment. And then she had claimed Rocío had embarrassed *her* in front of her friend by turning down a position she had never asked for.

A perdido assistant position in a politician's office. It was a time-honored system of political apprenticeships, generally reserved for family members and close family associates. Rocío was neither, and in that position, she would either have to fight viciously for every opportunity or beg for crumbs. *That's what my mother wants for me?* Her jaw ached from clenching it so hard. *Why do I let her do this to me every time?*

Her own response had been less than satisfying. She had told her mother she'd stop responding to her messages if she kept doing this, but they both knew it for an empty threat.

The sight of a friend's strained, gray face abruptly pulled Rocío out of her thoughts. María Paz looked straight through Rocío, her eyes shocky. Her teeth worried her bloodless bottom lip.

"Maipa?" Rocío reached for her arm. "What's wrong? Can I help?"

María Paz focused on her and jerked back. "Rocío, I can't—excuse me." She rushed away, careening off a chaski, sending his stack of newspapers fluttering to the ground. The boy shouted a curse after her, and Rocío bent to help him collect the papers.

After he hurried away, Rocío unwrapped a piece of gum and surveyed the street. On one side, the sign for the gossip rag *Oye* glittered in gold script. On the other, an accountant's somber font read BETEN AND DAUGHTERS. Had Maipa just exited one their offices?

A brief conversation with the accountant established that Maipa had not visited their establishment. That left the gossip rag, a disturbing prospect. Inquiries there might get Rocío or the CJC on its front page; she wanted that about as much as an actor wanted to forget her lines on opening night.

Back at the CJC, Espinoza pounced on Rocío as soon as she walked in. It was much quieter than it had been an hour ago. "Chief Oshinsky wants to see you."

"Right now? Just me?" Rocío asked.

"Yup."

"Do you know what about?"

"She didn't say." Espinoza shrugged.

Rocío left her coat in the locker room and took the stairs to Oshinsky's office. Her assistant, Paloma Faro Otxandabaratz, gestured her in, perhaps a tad more gracefully than usual. Rocío wasn't sure what that meant.

"Close the door, please," Oshinsky said. She had fine graying brown hair pulled into an unadorned bun that Rocío's mother would have frowned at and calloused hands her father would have lifted his eyebrows at ever so slightly, had they ever met Oshinsky. They would have noticed the intelligence in her blue eyes, but without the outward packaging cared for to their standards, they would have dismissed it. And they'd have failed to see the humor in them entirely.

"What's up?" Rocío slung herself into the armchair on her side of the desk and glanced at the altar to Oshinsky's ancestors on top of the bookcase. Sometimes it held a clue to her concerns, but today it was the usual marigolds, candles and photos of her parents.

"I want you to do something for me."

"Of course." Rocío sat up straight and reached for her notepad and pencil. The last time Oshinsky had asked her to do something with that tone of voice, it had involved a tacata music contest, embezzlement and black market turkeys. In other words, it hadn't been boring.

"Not like that." Oshinsky steepled her fingers, the paleness of her eyes, a rarity in this city full of brown-eyed citizens, still disconcerting after all these years. "Paloma is smart and quick thinking but also methodical."

"Yes?" Rocío asked, confused but willing to go along.

"She also wants to be an advocate and eventually a detective."

"She'd be a good one—she's sharp, like you said," Rocío said, finding her place in the conversation. "Doesn't miss a lot."

"Which is why I want her to start field training with you."

And she lost it again. An annoyed flush heated Rocío, and she shifted, wishing she hadn't worn a wool sweater. The image of Paloma's perfectly coifed hair and perfectly composed face rose in Rocío's mind. Her pulse pounded in her ears. Unlike Oshinsky, Paloma was perfectly smooth, perfectly elite. She was exactly what Rocío's parents wanted Rocío to be, exactly what she didn't *want* to be. Every model her parents wanted her to emulate looked like Paloma. Rocío could and did deal with people like her every day, but at a distance. Then she came back to the CJC and got away from them. Training Paloma meant she would never get away. It would be like having her mother hanging over her shoulder.

Seres celestiales, Paloma was probably angling to be chief after Maurata and be Oshinsky's boss. Her family was closer to the top of the social hierarchy than Rocío's, but only just. In that position— their shared position—it was your duty to improve the status of your family. Rocío's refusal to do so was the main source of the friction between her and her family.

Being the chief of an important community justice center like Miraflores, which lay at the heart of La Bene's government district, was a prime stepping stone into politics. Those positions went to the people with connections, not the ones who did the hard work, like Deputy Chief Oshinsky; she would never be chief, because she was third-generation Benerex with no ties to the founding families. She had worked her way up to the rank of deputy chief. And what had Paloma done to deserve a promotion? Been born to the right family, that's all. Didn't Oshinsky see that?

"Oh. Are you," Rocío cleared her throat, "sure about her?" That sounded sincere, right? Not passive-aggressive? Or just aggressive?

"If she wanted to stay my assistant, I would keep her forever, but that's not what she wants."

And Oshinsky helped her people get what they wanted. Look at Rocío, one of Oshinsky's many protégés; look at half the forensic techs and chaskis who had become a regular staff member at the CJC. And now Oshinsky wanted to nurture a social climber into a position of authority over her and the whole CJC, never mind sticking her in the middle of Rocío and Hala's partnership. It made her feel sick.

But there were some things you didn't say right out to the boss, not even the best boss. Like, *I think you're being hoodwinked by someone you trust.* That took finesse that Rocío currently didn't have. Planning.

"I don't think I'm the best choice for this." There, that sounded reasonable, although it didn't actually address the problem. "I haven't trained a new advocate before, not from start to finish."

"It's time you did," Oshinsky said cheerfully, with no sign that Rocío's hints had landed. "Hala will help you. And I'm here to answer questions and support you. You're one of my best, Rocío."

Usually Oshinsky's hard-earned praise made Rocío proud, but now she just felt resentful. "But maybe not the best for *this*." And then she stalled, because who would be the best at protecting Oshinsky from herself? Not the other Díaz. Not Fede or Leo or Felix or Julia, the other detectives. "You could ask Hala." Even as she said it, she knew Hala's abilities lined up with Rocío's priorities, not Oshinsky's. So it wasn't likely she would say yes. And Paloma would still be right there.

"Paloma's strengths are similar to yours. She's good with people, and she's good at reading them. I want you to do it."

Rocío blinked and looked away from Oshinsky's direct gaze. She wanted to say no. But what reason could she give? *I don't like her* didn't hold water. You didn't have to like someone to work with them. And Rocío wasn't, quite, willing to have a tantrum and lose Oshinsky's good opinion. But she didn't want to train Paloma, work with her every day for months, give her advice, bring her into her metaphorical family and then watch Paloma destroy that family. *Get a grip, Chío,* she told herself. *This isn't a play.*

The desk didn't hold an answer. Neither did the framed photograph of Oshinsky's son and daughter. "Chief ..."

"Good." Oshinsky rapped her knuckles on her desk and startled Rocío into looking at her. "I want her to start immediately."

Rocío tried to resign herself to her fate. "Right. Anything else?"

"Just my thanks."

Paloma wasn't at her desk when Rocío left Oshinsky's office. *Reprieve.*

Rocío rushed down the back stairs. She found Hala with Yaco Tuz, a forensic tech, in one of the labs, explaining something about wood.

"There you are," Hala said. "I was wondering if I needed to send in the rescue team."

"Very funny."

"The Department of Transportation—"

"We have to go," Rocío said, snagging Hala's sleeve. "Sorry, Yaco."

He half lifted his hand to wave, but Rocío steered Hala to the back exit before he could finish.

Hala twitched out of Rocío's grasp and eyed her thoughtfully. "I need my coat, and so do you. It's raining again."

"Fine." Rocío reversed direction, but rather than cutting through the internal courtyard, where they'd be more visible, she led Hala the longer way around the back of the building, past the labs and along the edge of the big open office where the advocates worked.

She scanned the room and spotted Paloma facing away from them, next to Hala's and her desks. Rocío focused on the locker room door, blocking out everything else on the theory that if she didn't look at Paloma, Paloma wouldn't look at her. Once inside, she hustled them both into coats, used a small spark of magic to short-circuit the alarm on the emergency exit and pushed Hala out. She took the time to make sure the door closed tightly, which would reset the alarm, then hustled Hala down the alley.

"What did Oshinsky want?" Hala asked.

Rocío turned up her collar against the drizzle and didn't speak until they had reached the main street. "I hate this part of autumn. Hola, Señorx Romero," she called to the older woman sweeping leaves off the doorstep of Café Storia. "Is your son sick again?"

"He is, but how did you guess?" Señorx Romero leaned on her broom, brows arched in question.

"He usually does the sweeping," Rocío obliged her. "And also the doctor's assistant has been gossiping again. He's trying to impress one of the chaskis at the CJC."

"You hear everything, don't you? I've never seen such a talent for keeping gossip straight."

"Ouch. That's a little harsh."

"No, no," Señorx Romero said. "It's a good thing in a detective. Come for lunch. Ravioli with squash and walnuts."

"Are we having lunch? You never did explain where we're going," Hala said, sliding a look at Rocío.

"We're—"

"Detective Díaz," Paloma called. "Detective Haddad." She practically bounced up to them, smiling pleasantly.

"Hello, Paloma, what are you doing here?" Hala asked.

That was the thing about Paloma—she was always pleasant. The expensive gold and red silk wrappings in her shiny black hair were always evenly spaced and studded with gold or silver pins inlaid with lapis or amethyst. Her face was a perfect oval; even her earlobes were perfect. She reeked of privilege and pleasantness and she was a very good assistant. Rocío had always admired her competence until now. From an uninvolved distance. She really didn't want all that pleasantness up close and personal.

"Deputy Chief Oshinsky sent me. She says I'm ready for field training in support of my request to become an advocate, like you. I'm excited to be working with you. Thank you so much." She exuded sincerity and eagerness.

Rocío studied her, looking for signs that Paloma knew she'd been purposefully left behind. The elite of La Bene had grace and body control drilled into them, through years of etiquette classes, to mask their emotions, but Rocío had attended the same classes at her parents' insistence. Paloma's chin might be a little too high, her voice a little too forceful, but that could be nervousness.

"I'm excited for this opportunity," Paloma gushed.

"How wonderful," Rocío said more flatly than she intended, and then winced internally at her own lack of grace in comparison to Paloma. But Rocío was determined not to be taken in by her. If Oshinsky wasn't going to be careful, Rocío would be careful for her.

Paloma's smile faltered, and Rocío became aware of Señorx Romero still leaning on her broom, watching them.

"Well done," Hala said, with all the warmth Rocío hadn't been able to summon. "I didn't expect you to break with your family's expectations for another four months. Rocío is an excellent choice of mentor. You have a lot in common."

Rocío and Paloma broke off their staring contest to stare at Hala instead.

"What? I have people skills, even if Rocío always gets all the credit."

When Hala did use her people skills, they were often aimed at preventing Rocío from saying things she shouldn't. Like now.

"So where are we going?" Hala asked. "I assume the chief sent you."

"Right." Paloma almost visibly pulled herself back on topic. "The manager of La Valle reported a theft, and Chief Oshinsky is sending you. Us."

"Señorx Romero, will you save some of that ravioli for us?" Rocío asked.

"Of course. Anytime." Señorx Romero resumed sweeping.

"Ready?" Hala asked. "Rocío?"

"I'm ready," Paloma said with more peppiness than the situation warranted.

I'm not. "Let's go." Even to her own ears, Rocío sounded as sullen as the teenagers that morning. An annoyed detective, an overeager, unwanted advocate-in-training and the volatile world of one of the most famous performance spaces in La Bene. What could possibly go wrong?

Get a copy of Shadow of the City at your favorite retailer

PLEASE LEAVE A REVIEW!

If you enjoyed this book, it would be fantastic if you would leave a review!

Reviews prove to other readers that this new author is worth taking a chance on, help a book's rankings, and even determine whether an author can do some kinds of advertising. It would not be exaggerating to say that reviews make or break a book. If you take the time to review Shadow of the City, you will have my eternal thanks and gratitude and it will make it easier for me to keep writing books.

Please consider leaving a quick, honest review (it doesn't have to be long) on the review page where you purchased this book or on Goodreads or on BookBub — or all of the above!

Thanks so much!

R. Morgan

ALSO BY R. MORGAN

Writing as R. Morgan

Between the Mountain and the Sea

Rocío and Hala novels

River of Lies

Shadow of the City

Writing YA fantasy as Raf Morgan

The Desert Wall

The Red Fortress (coming soon)

The Far Oasis (coming in 2022)

Edited by Raf Morgan

Swift the Chase: Scenes from 9 Fantastic Stories

ABOUT THE AUTHOR

R. Morgan is a New Yorker living in Bangkok, Thailand. She works as a technical editor and was a Spanish to English translator for ten years. She has worked in Bogotá, Mexico City, Lima, Montevideo, Moscow and Surabaya.

She has protected sea turtles in Costa Rica, walked 11 dogs at once in Prospect Park in Brooklyn, and worked in district courts with victims of domestic violence.

She's a graduate of the Viable Paradise XVI writers' workshop and attended Rebecca Stead's 92nd Street Y workshop.

Her favorite things are long rambling walks, preferably under trees, but a city will do, the smell of rain and a good book.

She also writes YA fantasy under the name Raf Morgan.

www.ingramcontent.com/pod-product-compliance
Lightning Source LLC
Chambersburg PA
CBHW061231170626
46809CB00007B/2615